Wild Boys

–Heath–

EVERYTHING'S NAUGHTIER AFTER DARK...

Billionaires After Dark Series

Melissa Foster

ISBN-13: 978-1-941480-16-8
ISBN-10: 1941480160

Cover Design: Elizabeth Mackey
Cover Photography: Sara Eirew

WORLD LITERARY PRESS
PRINTED IN THE UNITED STATES OF AMERICA

A Note to Readers

My fans have been asking for a darker, sexier version of the Bradens, and I'm proud to bring you the Billionaires After Dark, written in the same raw, emotional voice as the Bradens and my other romance series, with naughtier language and amped up heat levels. These smoking-hot billionaires move fast, love passionately, and fall hard. If this is your first Melissa Foster novel, you have a whole series of loyal, sexy, and wickedly naughty heroes and sexy, sassy heroines to catch up on in my Love in Bloom romance collection (Snow Sisters, the Bradens, the Remingtons, Seaside Summers, and the Ryders). The characters from each series make appearances in other Love in Bloom books. There is a complete book list in the back of this novel.

Be sure to sign up for my newsletter so you never miss a release!
www.melissafoster.com/newsletter

Melissa Foster

For Les

Chapter One

FUCKING PERFECT. THOSE words played over and over in Dr. Heath Wild's mind as he thrust his tongue deeper into the receptive mouth of the sexy woman who was grinding her hips against his cock in the elevator of the Gray Mountain Lodge. He buried his hands in her hair and gave a less-than-gentle tug, testing the woman's boundaries. The sexy moan that followed was all the green light he needed to press her up against the wall and pin her wrists above her head with one large, capable hand, while thrusting his other beneath her little black dress and into her—*thong, hot damn*—beneath. He didn't waste any time finding his way inside this beautiful, willing creature. Her head tipped back, and he claimed her neck, sucking as he fingered her hot, wet center.

"Oh God. Yes. Right there," she panted.

Acutely aware that the elevator was about to reach the sixth floor, he circled his thumb over her swollen clit as he claimed her mouth in another ravishing kiss. She clawed at his dress shirt, making sounds that had him picturing her spread-eagle on his bed, arms restrained, with his face buried between her legs.

"Ah. Fuck." She dug her hands into his thick hair as the orgasm gripped her—and the elevator chimed.

Heath casually fixed her dress, unhurried by the elevator doors sliding open. He drank in her flushed cheeks, the light sheen of sweat on her upper lip that he wanted to lick off, and her full, heaving breasts.

"Open your eyes, sweetheart," he said in a gravelly voice. He wanted more, and he was about to get it.

ALLYSON JENNER TRIED to act nonchalant as she passed an elderly couple in the hallway on the way to her room, hoping they didn't smell sex wafting around her and the incredibly hot guy she was with. She lifted her chin as she unlocked the door, acting as if her hands weren't shaking, like she did this type of thing every day, as the mind-blowing kisser she was about to fuck obviously did. She might not do it every day, but she wasn't a stranger to hooking up with random guys, either. She enjoyed sex the way others might enjoy an occasional swim in the ocean: reveling in the shocking experience at first, then giving in to the exquisite pleasures, and finally, when she was satiated, going back to her normal life feeling rejuvenated for the next few months.

The door clicked shut, and the sound of the dead bolt sliding into place brought her back to the handsome man licking his lips. His piercing blue eyes raked over her body, lingering on her breasts. The edges of his mouth quirked up as he loosened his tie and cracked his neck to either side. Her nerves prickled. This was the moment she had to push past—the urge to flee from fear of the unknown. What if he was a psychopath? What if the staff found her bloodied body in the bathroom tomorrow morning? She'd watched him all afternoon at the medical conference downstairs. She hadn't missed that, while she'd been sizing him up, he'd been stalking her like prey, and it had turned her on before he'd even bought her a drink after the conference. She really should have gotten his name. What had she been thinking?

She knew exactly what she'd been thinking, because the thought had only grown more intense with every passing minute. She wanted to feel his powerful body above her, his arms around her, and the enormous cock bulging beneath his zipper and outlined by his dress pants inside her.

He clutched her hips and tugged her against his expensive suit, taking her in another mind-numbing kiss. She fumbled with the buttons on his shirt, desperate to get to the smattering of chest hair she'd seen peeking out of the top. She could feel the strength of him in his kiss, in his grip, in the rock wall behind her hands. He was easily six two or six three. She was five five, maybe five eight in her heels, and he—*what's his name?*—still had several inches on her.

"What's your name?" she asked between kisses.

"Heath."

Heath. She liked that. Smooth and hot, like him. She'd always loved a man's man. A man who made her feel feminine but didn't treat her like she was a delicate flower. A man who took what he wanted but still made her feel special, and this guy had stroked her hand, not her thigh, when they were in the bar. His eyes read, *I'm going to fuck you hard,* but his actions told her he knew how to respect *and* pleasure a woman. Crazy, she knew, because how much could he respect a stranger he was about to fuck? But if he'd put his hand on her thigh in public, it would have sent a completely different message.

"Ally," she offered.

The edges of his mouth curled up, but his eyes turned midnight dark as he tore her dress over her head, tossed it on the chair, and pulled her against him again.

"I cannot wait to get my mouth on you, *Ally*. To taste your come and feel you shatter against my tongue."

Her insides caught fire. If he could make her come with his fingers in less than a minute, she could only imagine what he could do with that viperous tongue of his.

Breathe, Ally. Be patient.

He rubbed the pad of his thumb over her bottom lip and ground his hips against hers, sending *patient* out the window.

"I want to feel your luscious lips wrapped around my cock."

His voice was liquid lust, and it was all she could do to whisper, "Yes."

She clawed at his shirt, the button of his trousers, his tie, desperate for him to fulfill his promise. He grabbed her wrists and trapped them by her hips.

"You in a hurry?" He lowered his mouth to her neck and sucked.

Yes. I want you inside me. "No." She squeezed her thighs together to try to satiate the longing between her legs. Every suck and stroke of his tongue made her nipples harder—if that was even possible. Good Lord, he was going to make her come again without even touching her below the waist.

He stepped back, assessing her body with those lust-filled eyes again, pinning her in place as they slowly dragged over her.

"You're fucking beautiful, *Ally*." Her name slid off his tongue like a sensual promise. He took his time stripping off his trousers and dress shirt, leaving his tie loose around his neck and his black Calvin Klein boxer briefs covering his enormous erection.

Heat thrummed through her at his casual striptease.

"Heath what?" The question was driven by nerves.

His confidence was titillating, the way he languidly laid his dress shirt over the back of the chair, then did the same with his pants. He stopped mid-move, pulled his shoulders back, and eyed her skeptically. In the space of a breath, Ally drank in his five-o'clock shadow, which gave him an edgy aura. His skin pulled taut over his handsome, squarish face and strong jaw. He had full lips, and his mouth was slightly small—though she already knew it gave great pleasure. He turned, squaring his broad shoulders, and her eyes dipped south, to the perfect planes of flesh before her.

"I'm not looking for anything more than tonight, Ally. No last names, no talk of what we do for a living. Just a night of intense pleasure. Are you okay with that?" He lowered his chin, and his eyes implored her to answer.

"Yes," she said with confidence. That's what she'd been assuming anyway. Nothing new there, but hearing the words made her feel a little...something. *Cheap?* No. Definitely not. They brought a rush that was even more powerful, more enjoyable.

His cock twitched beneath his briefs as he stepped closer, leaving only a sliver of space between them. She raised her eyes and met his hungry gaze, unable to stop thinking about the tie dangling from his neck.

"Good, because while I would leave you, I really don't want to miss out on experiencing you." He paused long enough for that suggestion to sink in. "I'd really like to tell you to get on your knees so I can see those luscious lips sucking my cock, but I'm a gentleman." He ran his knuckle down her cheek.

She closed her eyes with the intimate touch. Her knees were about to give out when he put his hands on her waist, and she opened her eyes.

"You still with me?" He stepped in closer, rubbing his cock against her thigh.

She nodded, swallowing hard against the urge to—God, she didn't even know what. Kiss him, suck him? Lick those incredible abs?

He lifted his chin toward the bed and raised his dark brows, then pressed a hand to her lower back. He guided her to the bed and came down over her, wasting no time in possessing her mouth again with his eager tongue. He fisted his hands in her hair, tugging just hard enough to sting, a scintillating mix of pleasure and pain. She rocked her hips against his hard length and he returned the movement, creating delicious heat and friction between her thighs. She wrapped her legs around his waist, wanting more, needing more, as his mouth found her neck again. *Oh God—her neck.* He released one hand, keeping the other hand fisted in her hair and holding her in place, he slid his fingers inside her thong again and he stroked her wet folds. With a tug of her hair, he wrenched her neck back as he buried his fingers deep inside her, stroking her into a furor of need. She writhed beneath him as his mouth wreaked havoc with her brain, licking and sucking his way over her collarbone to her breast. He teased her through her bra, then bit down, sending shocks of pleasure rippling through her. Her eyes slammed shut.

"Come for me, Ally."

He bit down again and she cried out as her body spiraled out of control. Her hips rose off the mattress, and light exploded behind her eyes as the most intense orgasm she'd ever experienced tore through her.

"You're so fucking hot. So fucking wet."

He buried his tongue in her mouth again. She couldn't

breathe, still trying to recover from the orgasm that hadn't yet fully eased. He breathed air into her lungs, and when he withdrew his fingers from inside her, she whimpered with need.

He stroked himself through his briefs, once, twice, along his hard length, making her salivate for it. For him. His eyes narrowed as he met her gaze.

"Fuck, Ally. That was incredibly sexy."

He stroked himself again, then came down over her and kissed her softly. It was a kiss of lovers, not strangers, and she found herself getting lost in it. In him. He smelled of leather, spice, and sex, and she rocked into him again, needing more of him.

He bit her lower lip and pulled gently as their mouths parted. Then he dragged the finger that had been inside her over the tender spot. Her scent, her taste, lingered on her lips. When his tongue swept over the same path, she nearly came again from the dirtiness of it all. Her mind was foggy with desire, and when he slid the tie from around his neck and looked down at her, she had a fleeting thought that maybe she should be scared. He might choke her. She didn't even know his last name, after all. But she wasn't scared. She was fucking turned on.

"May I?" he asked.

She trapped her lower lip between her teeth and nodded, having no idea what he was thinking.

He smiled. "Have you done this before?"

"No, but I haven't been to Coney Island or a zoo either, and I know I'd love them."

"You just got impossibly sexier." He brought her hand to his lips and pressed a kiss to her palm, then ran his tongue up the center.

She shivered as he wrapped the silk around her wrist, his

eyes never leaving hers.

"Okay?" he asked in a tender tone riding on restrained desire.

She nodded again, unable to find her voice. She'd never been tied up before, but she'd thought about it. A lot. He lifted her hand over her head and then reached for the other, raising his brows in question.

Her mouth went dry as she nodded. The kindness of ensuring her agreement and his careful movements, partnered with the kinky desires, made him all the more alluring as he wound the silk around her other wrist and bound them together. His breathing came harder as he placed her bound hands on the pillow above her head, then sealed his lips over hers again. She lifted her hands, wanting to touch him, and he pushed them gently down to the bed and pulled away from the kiss.

Come back.

"Want it off?" He eyed her bound wrists.

"No," she whispered. "I just wanted to touch you." The desire in her voice was so thick she could practically taste it.

"Oh, you will. Trust me, you will."

He slithered down her body. His big hands cupped her breasts as he tasted the cleavage between, and groaned. It was a guttural, sexy groan that sent shivers through her body and a rise of goose bumps over her skin.

"You have incredibly gorgeous breasts."

Ally closed her eyes, soaking in the sensuality in his voice. He unhooked the front clasp of her bra and pushed the cups aside, then lowered his mouth and teased her taut nipple. Her body vibrated with need, building, burning inside her. The ache for more was too great. She couldn't stop the plea from coming.

"Suck it," she urged.

He groaned as he sucked first one nipple—*hard*—then the other, moving between them in the same glorious rhythm as his cock pressing against her sex.

"Yes, harder." She arched against his mouth as he grazed her nipple with his teeth. Her entire body pulsed with fire as he took her over the edge again.

Before she came down from the orgasm, he kissed his way down her belly and tore off her panties. He used his mouth, prolonging her pleasure and leading her to another incredible climax.

Straddling her hips, he took her in a rough kiss that sent every nerve ending to the surface. The taste of her was still fresh on his mouth as he cupped her cheeks and touched his forehead to hers.

"I want to fuck your mouth," he whispered.

"Yes. Do it." She couldn't wait to taste him.

He reached for the bindings on her wrists, and she shocked herself when she said, "Leave them."

His eyes widened, then narrowed as he stepped from the bed and stripped off his boxers. His cock was thicker than she'd imagined, long and beautiful. He came up on the bed beside her and gathered her in his arms.

"You've got to put your arms down or you'll hurt tomorrow." He lowered her arms, brushing his thumbs over her bound hands as he gently placed them in front of her, then propped up pillows behind her and lifted her into a reclining position. "You okay?" he asked.

His thoughtfulness only warmed her toward him. She nodded as he straddled her and stroked his hard length, inches in front of her mouth. She licked her lips, leaning toward him as he pressed his hips forward. She swirled her tongue over the sensitive glans, then lapped at the bead on the tip. He moaned and pressed his hands flat against the headboard, moving in closer, his knees straddling her waist, allowing her to lean back against the pillows as he moved in and out of her mouth in a slow, taunting pace.

"More," she said around the thick head of his erection, and opened her mouth wider.

He thrust in deep, meeting the back of her throat. She bobbed forward and back, lifting her bound hands to cradle his sac.

"Aw, fuck, Ally." His muscles flexed all over his body as she sucked and teased and felt him swell impossibly thicker in her mouth.

He drew out fast. "I've got to have you." He unbound her hands, and his eyes darted around the room. "Fuck." He shot off the bed and retrieved his pants, then dug a condom from his wallet.

Ally watched him sheath his shaft, and in two determined steps he was perched over her again. His inky lashes blinked down at her as the tip of his arousal touched her swollen sex. She spread her legs wider, pushing on the back of his hips as he claimed her mouth and thrust in deep at the same time, sending a shock of pleasure through her. They both went a little crazy, pawing and sucking, biting and thrusting. He fisted his hands in her hair again, then eased his grip, cupping her head.

"Come *with* me."

It wasn't a suggestion, and it took only a minute for him to strike the spot that shattered her control. She cried out his name as he ground out hers—*Ally*—and their bodies clung together until the last of their magnificent orgasms pulsed through them.

Chapter Two

HEATH SAT IN one of the conference rooms Saturday evening trying to focus on the physician giving the lecture, but all he could think about was the incredible woman he'd left in the wee hours of the morning after he'd come harder than he had in years. *Ally.* She'd asked him to stay the night, and waking up with her in his arms had been a tempting proposition. But he'd stuck by his motto: *Get in, get off, get out.* He'd been clear with Ally. No ties—at least none other than the silk, leather, or otherwise that fall into the bondage category. He was a partner in a busy medical practice; the last thing he needed was for some clingy woman to complain about him working too many hours. That was why he rarely dated, and only when he was away from New York City, where he lived and worked, did he allow himself casual affairs. Vermont was far enough away from New York that he felt safe from clingy fingers, but hell if he could get Ally out of his head, with her delicate face, high cheekbones, and adorable rounded chin—and those big brown doe eyes that gave her a hint of innocence.

Eyes that said, *Fuck me hard, but don't tell anyone.*

Oh yes, Ally had tempted him into behavior he rarely allowed himself to enjoy the first time he was with a woman. But there was something about the way she'd kissed him, like their mouths had been fucking for years, and the way she'd come in the elevator, open and anticipatory, moving her hips in practiced precision as he stroked the spot that took her over the edge fast and hard. Oh yes, all those things brought out that hidden side of himself. And he'd fucking loved it.

He checked his watch. Another half hour and the full day of lectures would be over. He shouldn't seek Ally out again, but he'd been looking for her between each lecture and then again at the lunch and dinner breaks. Yesterday she'd been working at the registration desk when he'd arrived, handing out name badges and itineraries, and she'd been milling about between lectures. But he had yet to find her today, and it was driving him crazy. Had she left the conference early? He found himself wondering what she did for a living. She obviously wasn't a doctor, or she wouldn't have been handing out registrations. Maybe she worked for the hosting organization.

What was he doing? She was a one-night stand. He needed to leave her as such. He forced himself to push the lingering questions away.

The woman next to him had been flirting with him for the past hour, and even that hadn't distracted him from thoughts of Ally. Now she leaned in close, her slim shoulder brushing his.

"Want to grab a drink after the lecture?" Her husky voice slid over him.

He shifted his eyes to the blonde. *Dr. Arter*, she'd told him, as if he'd cared. She didn't know she'd already broken his cardinal rule. No last names. Her hair was pinned up in a tight bun. She wore a low-cut silk blouse that did nothing to mask her eager nipples, a tight black skirt, and a pair of expensive heels. She had the whole librarian thing down pat. Heath imagined she'd be a tigress in the bedroom. Just his type. He ought to do her just to get Ally out of his head.

He opened his mouth to answer and turned at the sound of the door in the back of the room creaking. His breath caught as Ally walked in wearing another short black dress. This one had lace sleeves, which seemed out of place for a medical conference, but it was sexy as hell. She carried a stack of papers right past him down the center aisle. He inhaled her scent as she walked by. Her perfume was sweet and floral, as it had been last night…until it had been overtaken by the scents of sex.

As she set the papers down on the table at the front of the room, she moved professionally, almost invisibly, though Heath imagined every man in the place was probably as hard as he was, watching her perfect ass and slim waist as she leaned over to push the papers farther across the table.

I'd like to bend you over that table.

He shifted in his seat to ease the tension beneath his zipper.

Dr. Arter must have taken his movement as an invitation. She ran the side of her heel up his calf, recalling his attention to her and reminding him she was awaiting his answer. Ally turned, momentarily scanning the attendees, and then dropped her gaze to the floor as she walked up the center aisle. A few feet from him, she lifted her eyes to Heath and slowed her pace.

"Well?" Dr. Arter asked.

Eyes trained on the beautiful woman in the center aisle who was currently turning a sweet shade of red, Heath answered, "Sorry. Not tonight."

He lifted his chin in Ally's direction, knowing she'd be reminded of the more enticing things they'd done last night. Her lips curved up, but then her eyes shifted to the foot pressing against his calf. Heath moved his leg away from the blonde's foot and winked at Ally.

She blinked several times, then hurried past him and out the door.

She was here after all.

She'd be his again tonight.

After the lecture, Terri, aka Dr. Arter, followed him out and stuck to him like glue, as he walked through the conference area looking for Ally, who had once again disappeared. He checked his watch. It was after eight. Late enough for a nightcap. Terri following him into the bar, rattling on about her orthopedic practice in Ohio and other things Heath had absolutely no interest in.

He slid onto a barstool, planning to bury his lust in alcohol.

Terri sat on the stool beside him and placed her hand on his forearm. *Christ.* Could he get a break? He was trying not to be rude, but hell if she couldn't take a hint. He flagged the bartender and ordered a gin and tonic.

"I'll have a sloe comfortable screw," Terri said with a seductive tone, eyes on Heath.

He couldn't help but smile at her innuendo. Of course, she had no clue that she was barking up the wrong tree. He was about as interested in a *slow, comfortable screw* as he was in a relationship. Heath paid the bartender and ran his hand through his hair, thinking of Ally. When the bartender returned with their drinks, Heath loosened his tie, gulped down his drink, and ordered another. He looked around the bar, and a bolt of memory-laced lust pierced his chest when his eyes landed on Ally sitting at one of the tables with two good-looking guys who seemed to be about her age, which, now that he was really looking, appeared to be in her midtwenties. Heath was thirty-four. Sleeping with anyone under twenty-five was probably crossing some sort of line that he didn't care to think about—especially if Ally slipped below that line.

The way her eyes were shifting around the room, and the tap of her foot, told him she was bored with her company. He didn't blame her. The guys couldn't look more vanilla if they tried. Khaki pants, white shirts, and haircuts that were a little too trendy. One look at their eyes told him of the inane conversation they were probably having, which he was sure rivaled the one Terri was thrusting upon him and he was casually not taking part in.

"So where did you say you worked?" she asked him.

His cue that it was time to leave. Heath sucked down his drink and motioned for the bartender.

"I didn't." This was the part of the night he loathed. Turning down a woman. He hated to hurt her feelings, and women could be so sensitive. He didn't want her to think she was unattractive simply because he wasn't interested. He could take her back to her room and fuck that tight little bun right off her head, but his cock wasn't the least bit interested. Nothing. Not a twitch of interest. He slid a glance at Ally again, and his whole body heated up.

"Oh, well. Where do you work?" Terri asked.

"Terri, you're a lovely woman, but I think I see someone I know. If you'll excuse me." He rose to his feet as the young male bartender approached.

"What can I do for you?" the bartender asked.

Heath slapped a twenty on the bar. "Send a screw me sideways to that young lady, please." He nodded toward Ally. The bartender smiled and nodded.

Terri turned on her heel with a huff and walked out of the bar. Heath breathed a little easier as he sank back down to the stool.

He watched Ally's eyes widen when the bartender brought

her drink. The bartender pointed to Heath, and Heath smiled over his shoulder.

She mouthed, *Thank you.*

He nodded, then turned to face the bar. If she came over, she was into another night of hot sex, and if she remained with Bore One and Bore Two, he was wasting his time. The fact that he cared and was hoping she'd appear beside him did something funky to his gut.

One more night. That was it.

At least that's what he told himself. She was hot as fuck in bed, and he wanted more. There couldn't be any other reason his skin prickled as she slid onto the barstool beside him.

"HEATH, ISN'T IT?" She lifted the glass, toying with him in the same way the screw me sideways had toyed with her. She'd thought about Heath from the moment she'd watched his fine ass walk out of her room at four that morning. She'd slept wrapped in his scent, which lingered on her sheets, pillow, and more potently, her skin.

"Interesting choice," she said, eyeing the drink before taking a sip and sweeping her tongue across her lower lip.

"I thought you might like that." His eyes lingered around her mouth, then shifted to the table where she'd left the two men. "I don't mean to ruin your fun."

A soft laugh escaped her lips before she could stop it. They were nice enough guys, but Ally couldn't date nice guys. She'd done that before and had quickly learned how boring too nice could be. Not that she wanted a bad guy or law-breaking guy, but she definitely preferred edgier men. And at the moment, the hunky, edgy man sitting beside her had her rapt attention.

"They're volunteering at the conference, like I am."

His eyes went serious and she knew he was banking that information, but when he shifted his eyes away from her, she realized she'd given him personal information that maybe he didn't want. He probably wasn't banking it but rather thinking about how she'd crossed his no-personal-information line. *Way to screw this up, Ally.* She'd promised herself not to nose through the attendee list to figure out who he was. Given the lecture he'd been attending when she'd seen him, she assumed he was a doctor. While other medical professionals attended the conference, they weren't as likely to attend the surgery-related lectures.

"Sorry. I forgot the 'no-personal-information' rule. Pretend I never said that." She sucked back the drink to numb the sting of knowing that he really had no interest in anything more than a one-night stand—*err…two-night stand if they went at it again*—and based on the narrowing of his piercing blue eyes, that's exactly where they were headed.

The side of his mouth curved as he reached up and touched the edge of her lip, then sucked the wetness from his fingertip. Her insides melted.

"Delicious. Would you like another drink?" He eyed her empty glass.

She leaned in close to his cheek and was assaulted by his scent, which her body remembered all too well. She felt her nipples harden as she whispered, "If I have another of these, you're going to *have* to screw me sideways."

"Well, now, sweetheart. We wouldn't want you to be under the influence while you're getting fucked sideways, would we?"

He rose to his feet, and she couldn't help but drop her eyes to see if he was as aroused as she was. Oh yeah. He was sporting a baseball bat.

A handful of people crowded in around them in the elevator. Ally and Heath stood in the back. She was disappointed. She'd been looking forward to a little mischief. She felt Heath's hand slide up the back of her bare thigh. She stole a glance at him, and he was staring straight ahead, as if he weren't running his fingers between her legs and driving her out of her flippin' mind. The elevator stopped, and when the doors opened, he slid his fingers inside her panties, then dipped them inside her. She clamped her mouth shut to keep from gasping too loudly and shifted her stance, sinking further onto his fingers. He stroked and plunged, relentless in his pursuit of her orgasm, and when she felt herself losing control, she turned her face away from the other people, pressed her mouth to his shoulder and bit down hard as the elevator came to another stop and more people got off—*including her*. She gritted her teeth as he withdrew his fingers, leaving her wet and horny, and—*finally*—the elevator opened on her floor. She walked past the remaining couples in the elevator, and for the second time in twenty-four hours wondered if strangers could smell sex as pungently as she did. The doors closed behind them, and in the space of a second Heath had her pinned against the wall beside the elevator, his cheek pressed to hers.

"Do you know how fucking hot that was?" He kissed her. Hard. "I nearly came in my pants like a teenager."

And just like that, she lost her ability to speak again. What was he doing to her? She'd never been so turned on in her life.

"Hey, you okay?" His tone was tender. He touched her cheek, and when she nodded without speaking, his eyes narrowed. "Did I cross a line?"

She shook her head. "Not one I didn't enjoy." He was so careful, so considerate, a complete contradiction to the edgy guy who had just finger-fucked her in an elevator full of people. His devilish grin revealed a playful side that she liked as much as the intense, sexual side.

"Come on, sweetheart. You can introduce me to your boundaries."

Chapter Three

HEATH LAY ON his back, enraptured by Ally riding his throbbing cock. Her long dark hair curled over her pert breasts. Her lips were slightly parted as she dug her fingernails into his chest. She was the most beautiful woman he'd ever seen, and whether he was buried deep inside her or pleasuring her with his hands and mouth, he wanted to be closer. It was an unfamiliar, insatiable urge that wasn't satisfied no matter how hard they fucked. He tried to skirt the confusing thoughts and focus on wanting to see her come apart again. He squeezed her nipples and was rewarded with a heady moan as she arched her back.

"Heath—" His name sailed from her lips like a prayer as the orgasm shuddered through her.

He sat up, holding her hips tightly as he kept up their frantic pace. She fisted her hands in his hair, and he took her breast in his mouth, sucking until he felt her inner muscles contracting again.

"Ohgodohgodohgod."

Her eyes slammed shut as he gave in to his own intense release.

He wrapped his arms around Ally and held her close, his cheek pressed to her breasts. Her heart beat fast and hard. He spread his hands across her back, soaking in the feel of her.

"Hey." She ran her fingers through his hair, drawing his

eyes up.

He was momentarily silenced by her flushed skin and her heavily lidded, soft gaze. "You really are a beautiful woman, Ally."

"I...Thank you." She ran her fingers lightly over his biceps, and a teasing smile played across her lips. "This feels an awful lot like cuddling."

He laughed. She felt too good for him to let go, but she was right. He was getting awfully close to crossing a line he didn't want to cross. He'd move...in a minute...or three.

"Not that I mind. I mean, it's nice being close to my mysterious lover."

"Is that what I am? *Your* mysterious lover?" For some strange reason, he wasn't cringing at the possessive statement. He shifted her onto her back and perched above her.

She giggled, and the sweet, sensuous sound gave him a warm feeling.

"Well, you are a mysterious man, and you are technically my lover, so yes, that's what you are." She touched his chin with her finger, then leaned up and pressed a kiss to it. "And you're still here five minutes after we did the dirty deed, which is four minutes longer than last night, so that feels like cuddling, too."

He liked this whole conversation a little too much, but it also rattled the hell out of him. He kissed her softly, knowing he was leaving tomorrow and wouldn't see her again. He was already mourning the loss.

What the hell?

"I don't cuddle." He pushed free from her arms and went into the bathroom to take care of the condom, wrestling with the desire to stay and do just that. When he returned, she was sitting on the bed with the sheet pulled up to her chest.

He fought the urge to climb under the covers and gather her into his arms. Reaching for his briefs, he said, "I'm leaving tomorrow."

"Where do you li—" She pressed her lips together. "Sorry. Right. Me too."

He stepped into his pants and reached for his shirt. "It's not you, Ally. It's my life. I don't have time for a relationship."

She swatted the air, as if she didn't care one way or another, but her eyes—her soulful, beautiful eyes—told otherwise. "Neither do I."

"I work a lot," he said halfheartedly.

"Me too." She sat up a little straighter, holding his gaze as he buttoned his shirt.

He sat on the edge of the bed to put his shoes on and wondered who he was trying to convince. "My life is crazy."

"Mine too. Crazy. No time." She shook her head, but she was leaning toward him, her sensuous lips an inch away.

"No ties." He said it more to remind himself than her.

"Except of the silk variety," she whispered.

Their mouths crashed together, causing them to tip sideways onto the mattress. He ripped the sheet from between them and filled his palm with her breast.

"I can't stay away from you," he said between heated kisses.

"No cuddling." She giggled.

He kissed the smile right off her face and moved off the bed. He gripped her behind her calves and pulled her to the edge of the mattress, then dropped to his knees and brought his mouth to her center. She buried her hands in his hair as he thrust his fingers inside her.

"God, I love the taste of you." He dragged his tongue up her inner thigh.

"Less talking, more licking."

"You're fucking incredible." He smiled as he lowered his mouth to her again. Over the last two nights he'd learned exactly how to touch her to make her body sing, and within seconds she was lost in another powerful orgasm, clawing at his shoulders and writhing against his mouth.

He kicked his shoes away, dropped his trousers, and came down over her, his hard cock pressing into her swollen sex. "Condom." He reached for his wallet and fished one out, then rolled it on and drove into her.

"Oh, God." She wrapped her legs around his waist.

"Too rough?"

"Hell, no."

Christ. He'd found heaven, and she came in a beautiful, smart package that he'd never see again once he walked out that door.

"I want your number." *Where the hell did that come from?* This was not a clean break. What happened to *Get in, get off, get out?* This was not at all what he was used to, but for some unknown reason, he didn't fight it.

Her eyes widened. "But you said…"

"No last names. No personal information. Just phone numbers."

She looked at him like it made no sense, and he knew it didn't, but he didn't want to walk out that door without some connection.

"Okay," she said softly.

He sealed his lips over hers again, taking her in a languid kiss. She moaned into his mouth, and he slowed his hips, taking his time and causing her head to tilt back.

"Oh. That's so nice," she crooned.

He kissed her again, feeling his chest tighten with the softened look in her eyes. He was used to fast, hard sex, not slow, careful fucking. *Slow, comfortable screw.* He'd knocked that idea to the curb hours ago. What the hell was he doing?

He sank into her harder, faster, drove in deeper, rushing through what was probably one of the best fucks he'd had since…well, twenty minutes ago, when she was riding his cock.

Holy hell. Recognition came with a shock of fear.

I feel something for you.

It had been years since he'd felt the unfamiliar constriction in his chest at the thought of leaving a woman and the desperate need for the ongoing connection. They were feelings he didn't particularly enjoy and had worked hard to suppress and finally move past until he had full control.

He couldn't look into her eyes. That was what had made him come undone a moment ago and ask for her phone number. He fought the urge and buried his face in her hair. She smelled so damn good. It was no use. He couldn't resist lifting his eyes and drinking in the rosy glow of her cheeks, the sweet bow of her lips—and the tenderness and passion brimming in her eyes. He felt himself falling into her.

He placed his hands on her soft cheeks and pressed a kiss to her forehead, tempering his movements and bringing her to a slow crescendo, keeping her at the peak. Her body contracted around him, her breaths became jagged, and as he took her in another soul-numbing kiss, his body shook and pulsed with another intense release.

Chapter Four

AFTER RETURNING TO her apartment in New York City Sunday afternoon, going grocery shopping, enjoying a brief jog, and trying futilely to stop thinking about Heath, Ally had called her older sister. It was eleven o'clock at night and they'd been talking for almost an hour. Ally had initially called to distract herself from thoughts of Heath, but she couldn't resist at least vaguely mentioning him to Amanda. Of course, once she'd started to talk about him, their conversation had gone a little deeper than *vague.*

"Are you going to tell me anything more about your mysterious lover?" Amanda asked. There was only thirteen months between them, and they'd always been close. Amanda had watched Fifi, Ally's blind cat, while Ally was in Vermont. Sharing a little of her tryst was the least she could do for her more conservative sister.

Ally pulled Fifi into her lap and petted her. "There isn't anything else to say. He made it clear that he was only interested in sex, nothing more, and I'm good with that." But that didn't mean she wasn't thinking about him endlessly and hoping he'd call. Okay, fine, so she wasn't exactly good with that. But it was all she had at the moment.

"Yeah, yeah. I get that. But he asked for your number, and you were there working the conference. Didn't you look him up?"

She pictured Amanda's dark brows knitted together as she meticulously ran through all the things Ally *should* have done. Amanda was a sharp paralegal who lived carefully, whereas Ally liked to live a little more recklessly in her personal life, though she was meticulous at work.

"No. I purposely didn't. Think about it, Mandy. He was at the medical conference, which means…."

"He's probably a doctor. Big whoop?"

Ally looked around her efficiency apartment. She could afford a slightly bigger apartment, but not having walls to navigate was easier for Fifi, and Ally was perfectly happy with her cozy space.

"It means his life is a world away from mine."

"What does that say about you, Al? That you think you're good enough to screw but not for anything more?"

"*I* screwed *him*," she pointed out. "I'm the one who said hello first. I think that counts."

"You're so weird. I'd say there was mutual screwing going on."

Ally heard the smile in her sister's voice.

"You're smart, you're funny, and you're hotter than any girl I know, Al. You can get any man you want. Why do you sell yourself short like that?"

Ally was starting to regret telling her about Heath, but she knew Amanda was just watching out for her. "I'm not selling myself short. It's not about not being worthy. It's about attitude. You know how I feel about doctors. Besides, this was just supposed to be a one-night stand. Fun, you know." She knew her sister was rolling her eyes, because Amanda always teased her about volunteering at medical conferences, where she was surrounded by doctors. But doing lab work *for* doctors and assisting at a medical conference where she had access to all of the transcripts and interesting medical information were two totally different things.

"Another weird generalization *and* pastime. Not all docs are like that."

"Oh, really? Do *you* work with doctors? They're arrogant, self-righteous egotists who think of the people in the lab as idiots." It had been Ally's experience at the laboratory where she used to work and at the hospital where she'd begun working a few weeks ago that most of the doctors weren't as kind and considerate as the other staff. She didn't even know if Heath *was* a doctor. Although if he was, he didn't act like she was any lower than him on the social ladder the way most doctors did. *Even after he found out I was volunteering at the conference and not attending as a medical professional.*

"No," Amanda said. "But my doctor isn't like that."

"Mandy, do you really think your doctor acts the same around you as he does around his staff? You're *paying* him." She leaned down and kissed the white spot on the top of Fifi's otherwise black furry head. "Besides, if I were looking for more, it wouldn't be from a one-night-stand."

"Um. Miss Hypocritical? You were a one-night-stand, re-member?"

Ally sighed. "I know, but long-term I want all the fun of quick and dirty sex with the warm, squishy feelings of love. I want to get tingly all over by the sound of his voice and know that every second we're apart, he's thinking of me."

"You want to be the heroine in one of my romance novels. I swear they get the best sex *and* the best guys."

"That would be nice. I'll take what they have." Ally laughed.

"Maybe you should give your doc a chance. If he's even a doctor."

"I don't know. It's not like I need *that* sort of conflict in my life. I had a great weekend, and tomorrow it's back to real life."

Amanda sighed. "Mondays suck. We should have lunch tomorrow." She worked around the corner from the hospital.

"Tomorrow?" Ally thought about what she had planned for the week, which was a whole lot of nothing besides work and catching up on a little reading. "Sounds good. Meet me around twelve thirty?"

"Perfect."

A call beeped through, and Ally's heart skipped a beat at Heath's name on her screen. "Oh my God. He's calling."

"And the mystery man unravels. Love you, sis."

Trying to ignore the nervous energy racing through her and sound casual, Ally answered Heath's call. "Is this the way we do the no-strings thing?"

He laughed. "Ally. I've missed your voice."

She closed her eyes tight, grinning like a fool, then forced her smile into an unemotional straight line and chased the excitement from her voice.

"Really? What else have you missed?" Fifi began to purr in her lap.

"Oh, are we going there?" His voice dropped seductively low.

She didn't have the courage to answer. Yes, she wanted to go there. It wasn't like she was going to see him again, and he'd already been up close and personal with every inch of her. What did she have to lose?

"Where are you right now, Ally?"

"Locations are off-limits, remember?"

"Ah, yes. I meant where in your place. Bedroom? Living room? Kitchen?"

"Oh." Why did that simple question turn her on? "Where are you?"

He laughed again. "I'm sitting on my leather couch in my living room with my shirt off and my pants unbuttoned. And, Ally?"

She was getting excited just thinking about him sitting like that. "Yes?"

"I'm thinking about you, so I'm hard as steel."

Her breath left her lungs in a rush at that visual. "Tie hanging around your neck? Because I find that sexy as hell."

"Don't tell me all your secrets, sweetheart."

She listened to him breathing, silently chiding herself for giving that up. She didn't know what the parameters were, and she realized that she didn't particularly care. Heath was like ice cream. She knew she should only have a little, but she couldn't resist overindulging.

"At least not all at once," he added.

She smiled.

"Ally?"

"Yes?" Silence stretched between them.

"What are you wearing?"

She glanced down at her boy shorts underwear and T-shirt and thought about lying. Her eyes drifted to Fifi. "Well, at the moment, I'm wearing a cute pussy"—she paused for impact—"cat on my lap."

"Ally, Ally, Ally. You are a dirty girl."

She mouthed, *Oh my God!* to the empty room.

"Tell me what you're wearing, Ally, and I suggest you put that little kitty down, because we're about to get a lot dirtier."

She set Fifi in her bed at the foot of the couch and lay back.

"Ally? Did you leave me?"

"No. I put Fifi down."

"Fifi." He paused, and she wondered what he was thinking. "Do you have any other animals?"

"No, just her."

"Where are you now, Ally?" he asked.

"On my couch."

"Lie down on your back and close your eyes."

Was she really doing this? Having phone sex with the guy she'd spent two nights having great sex with? The guy who wasn't giving anything up?

"I'll lie back if you tell me something about yourself."

He remained silent, and she prayed he wouldn't hang up.

"Heath?"

"I have three brothers," he offered.

She smiled and lay back on the couch. "Are they all as hot as you?"

"You're a little minx, aren't you? How about if we keep my brothers out of this conversation while I'm trying to seduce you?"

She closed her eyes. "Is that what you're doing? Seducing me?"

"Ally?"

"Hm?"

"What are you wearing, sweetheart?"

"A T-shirt."

"Bra?"

"No."

She heard him exhale. "And a pair of pink boy shorts."

"Those tiny, tight panties?"

"Mm-hm. Are you a fan?" She smiled at her ability to tease even though she was more nervous than she'd been in the hotel room with him. She'd never had phone sex before, but she enjoyed sex, and this brought a whole new level of excitement.

"I'm a fan of anything as long as it's on you. But I'm a bigger fan of you completely naked, lying spread-eagle with my mouth buried between your legs."

She inhaled a sharp breath and felt herself go damp.

"Ally? Is that short for Allyson?"

"Yes." She wasn't thinking, and it registered a moment later that he'd asked for her full name.

"I like that name. Allyson?"

"Yes." She sounded raspy, full of desire.

"Close your eyes and pretend I'm there with you." He paused, and she closed her eyes. "Are your eyes closed?"

"Yes," she whispered.

"Put your hand down your panties." He paused as she followed his instructions. "Are you wet?"

"Yes."

"Tell me what you feel."

"I'm hot and so wet. Swollen." Her embarrassment slipped away as she sank into the moment.

"Allyson, you know how to touch yourself like I touched you?"

"Uh-huh."

"I want to hear you come. Touch your clit, and tell me what you feel." He was breathing harder, and it spurred her on.

She stroked herself, feeling her climax building inside her.

"Allyson?"

"Huh?"

"I'm stroking my cock, thinking of you touching yourself.

Thinking about your hair spread out on the pillow and the way your tongue sweeps over your lower lip as you start to relax."

"Oh God." The image had her speeding up her efforts.

"I'm so hard, Ally. I wish your mouth were around my cock. I want to see your gorgeous eyes looking up at me when your mouth is full of me."

"I love your cock."

"Tell me more," he said in a low, gravelly voice.

She stroked herself as she spoke, remembering the feel of everything they did. "I love the feel of your cock in my mouth, the way your come tastes on my tongue. The way you fucked me."

"*Christ.*" She could tell he was gritting his teeth. "I want to fuck you now, Ally. I want to plunge deep inside you and ravage your sinfully delicious mouth as you come."

"Heath—" She arched against her hand, feeling her inner muscles contract around her fingers and unable to believe she was coming as he ground out her name and grunted through what she knew was his own intense climax. She listened to his heavy breathing, and strangely, she didn't feel embarrassed, but somehow felt closer to him.

"Sweetheart?" A gravelly whisper.

"Hm?" she managed.

"You're unlike any woman I've ever known."

She felt her heart swell with the compliment, though she knew it shouldn't. Phone sex and hot hotel sex were hardly a relationship. She pushed the hope away and quipped, "That's sort of like cuddling, isn't it?"

He let out a low laugh, and she heard him moving around. "Considering that I just came all over myself while listening to you come, I might admit to that."

"I've never done that before."

"I've seen you come, remember?" he teased.

"You know what I mean." She smiled as she went into the bathroom to clean up. "Phone sex," she said in a hushed tone.

"Me either."

She stopped cold. "Oh, please. You were too confident, too comfortable with it."

He laughed again, and it was a sound she was growing to like. A lot.

"Seriously. I haven't. And I didn't call to have phone sex with you. I called to hear your voice, but…"

"So you've never had phone sex before?" She sounded accusatory and hated herself for it.

"Is that jealousy I hear in your voice?"

Yes. "No." *This is so messed up. How can I be jealous of a guy I'm not even dating?*

"Allyson, there's one thing you should know about me. I never lie."

She rolled her eyes. As if she hadn't heard that too many times before to count. "You're a man. By default you lie."

"Ouch. That's a harsh generalization for a guy you just had phone sex with."

She smiled. "Sorry. I guess it is, but that's been my experience."

"That's too bad, sweetheart. But not all guys lie."

"Okay, let's not kill the mood." She leaned against the wall, not wanting to talk about her cheating exes. The last two guys she'd dated had both cheated on her, which was what had led her to more casual dating, if she could even call it dating. How hard was it to break up instead of cheating? She'd never understand that mentality.

"I don't like knowing that you've had a bad experience in

the past." The sincerity in his voice sent her sliding down the wall and sitting on the floor.

"Haven't we all had them?"

He was silent for a long moment. "Yes, I suppose we have."

"So, I guess girls suck, too."

"Not all, I hope," he answered.

She heard him opening up, and she wondered how much information he might share. "Living life on a hope and a prayer now, Heath?"

He sighed. "Aren't we all?"

"Who was she?" She closed her eyes, knowing he'd probably shut her down.

Silence filled the airwaves. She opened her mouth to say good night just as he answered.

"A woman I dated in college." He blew out a breath. "I caught her in bed with a buddy of mine. Well, a guy I thought was a buddy."

"Oh. I'm sorry. If it makes you feel any better, the last two guys I dated both cheated on me. I'm starting to think that monogamous relationships are for the birds." Fifi rubbed against her side, and she lifted her into her lap.

"Maybe. Although, my brother Logan met a woman, and they're happy."

She wondered if he realized he'd revealed another piece of personal information.

"That's good," she said. "So maybe there is hope for mankind." She lifted Fifi and kissed her head.

"Who're you kissing?"

"You heard that?"

"Yes. I hear every breath you take."

She leaned her head back against the wall as his words washed over her.

"Fifi," she answered.

"A loyal friend."

She smiled. "That she is. I found her in Central Park when she was just a baby. She was skin and bones. She's blind, and the most loving pet I've ever had."

"Central Park?" His voice grew serious. "Are you in New York?"

"Am I allowed to answer that?"

"Allyson, I asked; you can answer."

"Does that mean if I ask, you have to answer?"

He sighed. "I didn't say you *had* to answer. I said you *could* answer."

"Hm…" She toyed with him.

"Ally, do you live in New York?"

"Heath? Where do you live?"

He didn't answer.

She wasn't about to play this one-sided game, and she had no idea why it bothered her after what she'd just done with him. Maybe that was why. Or maybe it was her sister's voice ringing in her ears about putting herself down.

"This has been fun, but I have to go. Good night, Heath." Ally didn't wait for him to respond. She ended the call and blew out a breath, then lifted Fifi up and looked into her unsighted eyes. "Well, Fifi. I guess that's over. I deserve more than silence."

She took a warm shower, and when she came out, the message light on her phone was blinking. She read the text from Heath. *I live in the city. Good night, Allison.*

She wondered if he meant New York City, or if he was being vague. She smiled as she typed her response.

I live in a city, too. And it's Allyson. Good night, Heath.

Chapter Five

MONDAY MORNING HEATH arrived early to the offices of his orthopedic practice, NYC Sports Medicine, in the heart of the city. He'd given up sleeping around four that morning, went for a run through Central Park, hit the gym, and by seven he was sitting behind his desk looking out over the city and fantasizing about Ally. He hadn't expected to get dirty with her on the phone last night. He'd only wanted to hear her voice, but hell if she hadn't surprised him by initiating the dirty talk. Listening to her take herself over the edge last night had been as exciting as hell. It wasn't until afterward that he'd felt different, wondering what she was feeling after they'd hung up the phone and whether she'd been telling him the truth about never having had phone sex before. It wasn't something he'd dabbled in before. He'd thought he'd feel vulnerable, jerking off while on the phone, and he liked to be in total control. But with Ally, everything felt different, and his need for control eased.

He reread her text from last night for the tenth time that morning, wondering if she was in fact in New York City, or if she was just playing with him. He liked that snarky side of her, too, because she was snarky sweet, not snarky obnoxious, like some women were. She was the perfect blend of femininity, sensuality, and intelligence, and that was what had him sending her a text even though it went against his cardinal rule.

I thought about your lips all night. It was a very long night.

He set his phone on the desk and opened a patient file. His eyes darted back to his phone every few seconds. He glanced at his watch, wondering what she was doing, where she worked, and if she was thinking of him, too. Why had she volunteered at the conference? Was she linked in some way to the ortho field?

He tried to focus on one patient file after another, but his mind kept circling back to Ally. He wondered why she hadn't texted back, and he couldn't stop replaying last night's conversation in his mind.

A knock at his office door brought his eyes up. Before he could say, *Come in*, the door pushed open and his younger brother Logan sauntered in, wearing a pair of dark slacks and a crisp white dress shirt with the sleeves rolled up to his elbows. Logan was two years younger than Heath and a private investigator. For a moment Heath contemplated having Logan track down Ally for him, but he quickly nixed that idea. He wasn't a stalker.

The four Wild brothers looked strikingly similar; they were either six two or three, with broad shoulders, athletic builds, and thick dark hair. They got their blue eyes from their mother, whose eyes had changed to a grayish blue when she'd lost her sight during a home invasion, the same home invasion that had killed their father while he was trying to protect her; the home invasion that had taken place while Logan was on an overseas mission with the Navy SEALS. He'd returned home a broken man, having been fighting for his country while his father lay dying and his mother was savagely beaten.

"Logan. Everything okay?" Heath motioned to the chair across from him. He'd just seen Logan last night at dinner with their mother, as they had every Sunday night since their father was killed.

"You tell me." Logan leaned forward, elbows resting on his knees, and steepled his fingers beneath his chin. He raised his brows as if he had a secret he was dying to tell—or rather, knowing Logan, he suspected that Heath had a secret.

And Heath was definitely not itching to share.

Heath leaned back, locking his fingers behind his head, and shrugged. "Mom seemed well last night."

Heath had told Ally the truth. He was not a man who lied, not even to his brothers. His father, Bill Wild, had raised his boys to have strong family values. Honesty and loyalty topped the list. One would think that having such strong ties to family would lead the Wild brothers to long-term relationships, but that's where things went awry. Heath had been burned, and he wasn't interested in being burned again. He lived an honest life, which was part of the reason he had a no-ties rule. He didn't have any interest in getting into a relationship that might cause him to start acting in ways he didn't want to. He didn't want to be nagged into defending his actions, either. He was doing just fine sleeping with a handful of women when it suited him.

At least he had been.

Until Ally.

He shifted his eyes to his silent cell phone, wondering why she hadn't texted him yet. Again, he wondered why he cared.

"That was another reason I came by," Logan said, bringing Heath's mind back to the present. "I want to take Stormy to a Broadway show tonight. She's never been, and I was offered great tickets. Any chance you can stop by Mom's for me?" Logan was the first of Heath's siblings to fall in love, and he'd been the most likely not to. They'd all been surprised when he'd brought Stella "Stormy" Krane to their mother's house for dinner. Stormy had been on the run from an abusive, drug-trafficking ex-boyfriend, and Logan had helped her track down enough dirt on the guy to get him sent to jail for the next twenty years. Logan had fallen hard and fast for her, and Heath had never seen his brother look happier.

"Sure. I'm happy to stop by." Heath and his brothers took turns stopping by their mother's house on a nightly basis. They visited, took her out for groceries, to events and dinners. It was not only their way of making sure that losing her sight didn't mean losing out on other aspects of her life, but it was also a way for them to ensure she was protected and safe. Heath had spent many nights driving by at odd hours to check on her, and he knew his brothers did as well. Their mother had plenty of friends she spent time with, but nothing replaced family. Heath knew that no matter how often they visited and what gaps in her life they filled, nothing would ever replace the emptiness their father's death had left behind.

Heath's phone vibrated. He felt his pulse quicken and noted the unfamiliar sensation as he snagged the phone and read Ally's text.

Your body must have been burning. I had an X-rated dream about you last night.

He felt himself smile as he typed a return text.

What did you do about it when you woke up?

He set the phone down, and Logan cleared his throat. *Shit.* From the narrow-eyed look Logan was giving him, Heath knew he might as well have a tattoo on his forehead that said, *Yup.*

I've got a secret, and she's damn hot.

Heath pushed the files around on his desk and avoided Logan's curious gaze. "So, what else is up? I'll stop by Mom's tonight after I finish rounds at the hospital, but I've got to get started on my patients." He glanced at Logan, who had a shit-eating grin on his face. Heath shook his head.

"So that's how we're going to play this? First you show up for dinner at Mom's last night and check your phone about a dozen times."

"Patients."

"Uh-huh," Logan said. "How do you explain the smile you had plastered on your face last night? And just now, when you were returning that text, you had a look in your eye that I don't even want to try to decipher. Unless your patients have started blowing you, I'm thinking there's a woman involved."

"Logan." Heath shot him a narrow-eyed, warning stare.

Logan scoffed. "Heath, you think that look is going to stop me from asking about whoever this is?" Logan rose and paced, rubbing his chin with a serious narrowing of his eyes. "You went to a conference in Vermont, which we all know probably led to an anonymous sexual tryst."

Heath tried to keep a straight face and shrugged.

"Stormy said you were looking at us last night with 'puppy-dog' eyes."

"What the hell does that mean, Logan?" Heath rose to his feet.

"She says you were looking at us like you were thinking about what we had. Our relationship."

Heath picked up a file and flipped through it, trying to disguise the part of him that agreed with Logan. "No thanks. I was probably looking at how pussy-whipped you'd become."

The truth was, he had been trying to figure out how his brother had gotten lucky enough to snag a woman like Stormy, who adored the very ground he walked on and was strong enough to give him shit in equal measure. She was perfect for him. And sure, part of Heath began wondering if he might be able to find that, too. With Ally.

"Hey, don't knock it." Logan crossed his arms and lowered his chin. "And don't talk about Stormy that way or I'll kick your ass."

"That wasn't a comment about Stormy. I think the world of her. You know that. It was a comment about how much you've changed. You've gone soft."

"Only around her, and hell if that's not exactly who I want to be. What's wrong with you? You get a text and smile like it gave you a hard-on. Just admit there's a woman in there somewhere. My PI skills don't ever lead me astray."

Heath leaned both hands on the desk and bowed his head. When he lifted his eyes to meet Logan's again, he couldn't lie.

"Okay. Fine. I met someone. But don't get all sappy with me. I don't even know her last name, where she lives, or anything, and I prefer to keep it that way."

Logan arched a brow. "I can fix that in about ten minutes."

Heath ran his hand through his hair. "No thanks, Logan. What the hell do you want from me? I don't get it, okay? She's…She's different from other women."

Logan sauntered around the desk and patted Heath on the back. "Dude, welcome to the end of everything you ever believed about yourself. You're standing on the precipice of the rest of your life. Either walk the tightrope and see where you end up, or run like hell, because this middle-of-the-road shit doesn't work. I know. I've been there."

"*Pfft*. This isn't *that*." *Is it?* No, it wasn't anything like Logan and Stormy. They'd had a good time, a few amazing fucks. Great phone sex.

And the first real conversation I've had with a woman in years.

His phone vibrated with another text. Heath eyed it as Logan's mouth quirked up in another smart-ass grin.

"Patients are calling," Logan said as he waved and headed for the door.

Heath read the text from Ally as Logan left.

Wouldn't you like to know? What did you do about your long, hard night?

Holy fuck. Had he finally met his match?

He returned her text, wondering how far she was willing to go.

I took things into my own hands, wishing they were yours.

Heath gathered his patient files and was about to put his phone in his pocket when another text vibrated through.

If they were mine, you'd probably have them bound together. But I seem to remember you having an affinity for my mouth.

How was he supposed to see patients with a hard-on? He sent her a quick reply. *Your mouth is quite appealing, as are your hands and certain other parts of your body.* He wanted to see her, and at the last second, before sending the text, he added, *What city do you live in?*

ALLY STARED AT her cell phone, trying to decide how to

answer the text from Heath that had come in hours earlier. She'd been contemplating her response all afternoon. She had dreamed about him, and yes, she'd given in and pleasured herself rather than coming into the lab at the hospital where she worked sexually frustrated. Mondays were busy and frustrating enough. She didn't need that kind of added tension.

She'd been terrible company when she'd met Amanda for lunch. She'd spent the entire time debating telling Heath where she lived. She wanted to tell him she lived in New York City. Maybe he lived close by and they could see each other. But that *also* made her nervous. She could see how a man like Heath could be addicting, and she didn't know if that was a good or a bad thing.

Who was she kidding? *Become addicting?* She was already craving him like a cocaine addict craves another hit.

She decided to play it cool and see what happened.

I think we've stretched the definition of "no ties," which is a shame, because I kind of liked playing with your tie.

"Hey, Ally, do you have those results done yet?" She shoved her phone in the pocket of her lab coat as Marty Crolor came into the back room of the lab where she was working.

"Dr. Warton is on the warpath." Marty was in his late twenties. He'd shown Ally the ropes over the last few weeks since she'd started working at the hospital. He was smart, helpful, and almost always in a good mood.

"Yes. I've already submitted them. Nothing out of the ordinary." She went to one of the computers and pulled up the report she'd filed. They ran a tight ship in the medical lab. Busy from the second they arrived until the moment the next shift took over; running tests, delivering results, and drawing blood from patients was all in a day's work. Ally enjoyed every minute of her chaotic day. She'd come to work at the hospital from a private lab facility because she wanted more one-on-one interaction with patients. She knew how difficult giving blood was for some people, and Ally had a knack for helping patients feel at ease.

A printer spit out a document, and Marty pulled the order and looked at Ally with a quick raise of his brows.

"Want to do a peds blood draw?"

"Heck yeah." Ally's heart went out to all the patients, but she was especially touched by the children. She changed from her blue lab coat to the white one she wore on the floor, then grabbed the tray of supplies she'd need to draw blood as Marty read off the order, telling her which room, the patient's name, and the doctor who'd ordered the procedure. Marty rated the doctor a four on the fear-inducing scale they used in the laboratory to assess the doctors' attitudes toward the staff. A four meant that he was prone to nasty comments but did so calmly. In other words, he'd rip the staff to shreds while smiling, as opposed to a five, who was more like a rabid dog. Ally didn't like to deal with fives because it was difficult for her not to give them shit right back, and doing so would cost her her job. At least with a four she could tune out the words and focus on the smile.

On her way up to the seventh floor she debated telling Heath where she lived. At least that way they would know if seeing each other was even an option. Otherwise, how long would this game go on? She loved every second of it, but she was already feeling a little addicted to their naughty texts and hoping for more sexy calls. How would she feel if they did this for another week or two and then suddenly the calls and texts stopped?

She pushed away those thoughts and made herself stop thinking about texting Heath so she wasn't delayed in taking blood from the little boy, who was probably a nervous wreck.

She found the seven-year-old boy, Johnny Waselchec, watching television.

"Hey there, buddy." She smiled as she came around the bed and set her supplies down.

Johnny looked over with the widest blue eyes she'd ever seen and clutched his mother's hand. His mother slid a nervous smile to Ally.

Ally glanced at the television, determined to keep his mind off the needle.

"Cartoons? I wonder if my boss would mind if I watched with you for a while." She patted the mattress beside his legs. "Move over. I'll sit right here."

Johnny laughed.

"What? You don't think I should?" She wrinkled her brow.

"No," he said with another sweet laugh. "You have to work, not watch television."

Ally huffed. "This grown-up stuff is highly overrated. I'd much rather watch cartoons. But I guess if I *have* to work, I will. You don't have to work, though. Lucky for you, you can just watch that show while I work." By the time he looked at his arm, she'd already cleaned the area over his vein and was ready to draw his blood. She glanced back up at the television.

"Why don't you watch that show. Since I'm not allowed to watch, can you tell me what's happening? I hate missing cartoons."

Johnny blinked up at the television. "The dog is trying to catch the cat."

She heard a thread of fear in his voice and tried to ease his worry, knowing the needle wouldn't hurt too badly. It was usually the idea of the needle that hurt more than the stick itself. She'd often thought that if blood draws were celebrated instead of feared, children wouldn't be quite as afraid. *Hey, Johnny! You get to give blood today! Isn't that great?* But she assumed that by the time a child needed to have his or her blood drawn, the parents were too worried to think of such things, and she didn't blame them one bit.

"You're going to feel a little pinch, but don't worry— afterward you get really cool stickers. I'll give you two extra stickers if you keep telling me about the cartoon."

He smiled and relayed the cartoon as she took his blood. When she was done, he gazed up at his mom and said, "You were right, Mom. Only a little pinchy."

Johnny chose his stickers—four instead of two—and Ally thanked him for telling her about the cartoon before she headed back down to the lab. She changed her lab coat and resumed her work.

The afternoon passed without another text from Heath. Ally tried to convince herself that was a good thing. Really, how far could a relationship based on a few nights of hot sex and one act of phone sex really go? The closer it got to the end of her shift, the more annoyed she became with herself for checking her phone. When had she become so dependent? He probably had a handful of girls—or more—that he played these games with. She took out her phone and deleted the flirty texts.

No more sexy texts with a guy she hardly knew. God, what had she been thinking anyway? She'd have given Mandy hell if she were playing the same sexy games with a stranger. *Only he's not really a stranger.*

She groaned at herself for rationalizing the situation,

chalked it up to a momentary lapse in judgment, and tried to focus on her work. Not that she regretted a second of their time together, or the phone call, or the texts. No, the momentary lapse in judgment was for her inability to stop checking her damned phone and wishing he'd text or call again.

I'm so glad I'm done with that craziness.

Only losers have phone sex.

Even if it was a total turn-on.

Even if he is hotter than any man I've ever seen.

She put her hand in the pocket of her lab coat and felt her phone, wishing it would vibrate, and she knew she was already in too deep to shut off her thoughts that easily.

She was looking through a microscope, working on the last order she needed to complete before the end of her shift, when a familiar deep voice sent a shiver down her spine and a shock of heat between her legs. She raised her eyes just as Heath walked into the room. Wearing a white dress shirt and a tie, covered by a white lab coat, he was even more devastatingly handsome than she'd remembered. He looked taller, broader, but those intense blue eyes bored through her with the same animal magnetism that they had the first time they'd seen each other at the resort—and the second. And the third.

Her mouth went dry.

She stole a glance at the name on his lab coat—Dr. Wild—then forced herself to lower her eyes back to the microscope before she made a complete ass out of herself.

Holy shit. Dr. Wild? Are you kidding me? That sounded like a fake name. He *was* wild—there was no doubt about that.

Shit. Shit. Shit.

"Ally is working on your results right now, Dr. Wild." Marty touched Ally's arm.

She couldn't continue staring into the microscope and ignoring them. She braced herself for humiliation—sure Marty would read, *I've sucked his cock,* in her eyes, and sat up to face them.

"Ally, this is Dr. Wild. He needs his results." Before walking away, Marty added, "Ally, I have only *one* more thing for you before the end of your shift."

Ally wrinkled her brow, and it wasn't until Marty winked that she realized he was rating Heath.

One. He'd rated Heath a one. Thank goodness.

Her heart thundered in her chest as she drew in a deep breath and finally met Heath's gaze.

"Dr. Wild," she said in the most professional voice she could muster.

Heath's eyes never left hers as he moved in close, his chest brushing her shoulder.

"Allyson. I guess New York City isn't so big after all." His hushed whisper slithered over her skin, leaving a trail of goose bumps.

He smelled like strength and warmth, and when he nodded toward the microscope and said, "May I?" she wished he were asking if he could kiss her, despite swearing him off only moments earlier.

There was no swearing off Heath Wild. Just the sight of him did funny things to her entire body, not to mention the way it flustered her mind.

He leaned down and peered into the microscope. "Did Fifi get your tongue?"

That shook her back to the present. He remembered her cat's name?

"I…" *Get your act together.* She closed her eyes for a beat and forced herself back into her professional, work-appropriate demeanor. "There's nothing remarkable in the findings."

He continued looking through the microscope as silence stretched between them.

"I was just thinking about how this case has me all tied up." He rose to his full height and pinned her in place with a seductive stare.

Her insides churned, and all the good parts of her remembered all the good parts of him—and exactly how incredible they were together.

"Yes, well…" She lowered her voice, unable to stop from playing their dirty, flirtatious game. "It is a *hard* case."

His eyes slid around the busy laboratory. "I'd like you to *come*…" He put a hand on her lower back and guided her to the microscope as her knees turned to jelly. "Take a look at this."

His grin told her that he knew exactly what effect he was having on her. He had that damn lab coat on, so she couldn't tell if she was having the same effect on him. He moved to her other side, where the table shielded him below the waist from the eyes of the other employees, and pressed his hard length against her hip. There was no mistaking the effect she had on him. She looked into the microscope so her coworkers wouldn't be wise to the flames igniting between them. She was surprised they hadn't already lit the room on fire.

He leaned in close again and said, "Now I know."

She gazed up at him in confusion. "Know?"

"What city you live in."

She swallowed hard at the look of lust brimming in his eyes. "Yes, well. No strings, remember?"

He touched her back again, and she swore she'd have a third-degree burn from the searing heat of it. "No strings. Only ties." He straightened his tie as Marty entered the room again.

"Is everything in order here?" Marty's eyes ran between the two of them.

Ally felt her cheeks heat up and stepped away from the microscope, straightening the reports on the table in hopes of breaking the sexual tension that tethered her and Heath together.

"Yes. I've completed Dr. Wild's results."

"Yes, she's tied up all my loose ends." Heath smiled, and when his eyes moved from Marty to Ally, she felt her insides melt.

"Perfect. Ally will type up the report and get it into the system. Is there anything else you wanted to see, Dr. Wild?" Marty asked.

Heath straightened his tie again. "I may need to dig a little deeper, but for now I think these results are clear. Thank you."

Marty smiled. "Okay, well, I'll leave you in Ally's capable hands."

Don't I wish. Her fingers itched with anticipation.

"Now, that's someplace I'd like to return to," he said quietly.

"No ties," she reminded him.

"Right. Dinner, then?"

"Thought you weren't looking for anything more than…what we had." She didn't need to be the booty call of a doctor in the hospital where she worked. That had trouble written all over it.

"I wasn't." He held her gaze, and she read so many conflicting messages in his blue eyes that she could barely think straight.

"Then why?"

He shook his head. "I don't know."

Well, that's not going to win you a date.

He stepped in closer. "Maybe it's your beautiful brown eyes, or the way you challenge my smart-ass comments. Maybe it's the incredible sex. I don't honestly know, but I've thought about you every second since we met, and let me tell you, Allyson. It's hard as hell to be a good doctor when all my blood is residing below my waist."

She couldn't help the laugh and smile that brought. "Okay."

"Okay?" His eyes widened with surprise.

"Did I stutter?"

He shook his head and smiled, as if they were discussing the weather. "If we weren't in your workplace, I'd kiss that smirk right off your lips."

Yes, please.

Chapter Six

HEATH RACED OVER to his mother's house after work, stopping first to pick up a few groceries just in case she was running low. He hated rushing through a visit, but he wanted to get home and shower before meeting Ally. He pulled up in front of his childhood home and parked behind his brother Jackson's motorcycle. He wondered why Jackson was there. Jackson and their youngest brother, Cooper, owned a prestigious photography studio and rarely had free time in the early evenings. He knocked twice before walking into the living room of the cozy two-story home, where he found Jackson and his mother sitting on the couch. Jackson's black leather jacket lay on the couch beside him, and their mother's knitting needles were on the coffee table. Jackson rose as Heath came into the room.

"It's me, Mom. Hey, Jackson. How's it going?" Heath said as he set the bag of groceries on the coffee table and leaned down to hug his mother.

"Hi, lovey." His mother kissed his cheek. "What a nice surprise. Two of my boys here at once." She sank back down to the couch and patted the arm of the recliner beside it. Heath swore his mother had every inch of her home memorized. She'd refused to move after the attack that had left her blind and their father dead, insisting that nothing would chase her away from the home where she'd raised her family—the only home that had memories of her deceased husband.

"Not much has changed since last night," Jackson said. "I was doing a shoot around the corner and stopped by to see Mom. How about you?" Jackson was four years younger, an inch shorter, and had a penchant for the models and actresses he photographed.

"Good. Had a crazy day and I'm running late. Are you cooking dinner for Mom? I brought a few groceries, Ma. I'll put them away in a sec."

"I'm taking Mom out to dinner. Here, I'll put the groceries away while you visit for a minute, if you have time." Jackson grabbed the bags of groceries.

"You're taking Mom out on your motorcycle?" Heath arched a brow.

"We're walking around the corner to the café," Jackson said as he went into the kitchen.

Heath sat beside his mother. She was smiling, and she followed his movements as if she could see him. She reached over and patted his leg, fishing for his hand, which he happily placed in hers.

"You're running late? You don't have to stay and visit, honey." Mary Lou Wild was a kind and loving mother. She had shoulder-length dark hair, an olive complexion, and a smile always at the ready. After their father was killed, she'd fought her sons on their nightly check-ins, but she'd quickly realized that they were still as stubborn as they'd been as kids, and she'd given in to their need to watch over her.

"It's okay. I've always got a minute or two to spare," Heath said. "Did you have a nice day?"

"Oh, yes. Debra came by and we had a nice visit. Her son's

53

getting married in a few months, and she's over the moon." She patted her thick dark hair in a way Heath had seen her do a million times before, as if she were making sure it was still there. He imagined that even though his mother wasn't overly conscious about her looks—*Personalities reflect beauty, not hair and makeup*, she'd always said—it was disconcerting not to be able to look in a mirror every now and again. "Where are you rushing off to?"

Heath debated making up an excuse, but he wasn't a liar, and his mother had a way of seeing right through her sons' lies.

"I have a date."

"Oh. A date." She smiled, and Heath shook his head. "Well, that's different, isn't it?"

"Very," Heath answered.

"Well, then, she must be special. Maybe one day your great-grandmother's ring will be put to good use." She patted his hand and turned as Jackson came into the room.

The mention of his great-grandmother's ring surprised him. His father had given the ring to his mother when he'd proposed. On their fifteenth anniversary, he had bought her a new ring, and he'd told Heath that one day he'd find the woman he wanted to marry, and that as the eldest, he could give her that ring. Heath had forgotten about the conversation until just now.

"Who's the lucky lady? Anyone I know?" Jackson slid into the recliner.

"God, I hope not," Heath teased.

"Nice," Jackson said. "Seriously, who is she?"

"Sweetie, leave your brother be." Mary Lou used endearments like first names. *Baby, lovey, sweetie.* They answered to all of them. "If Heath wants to share that information, he will do so without you poking your nose into his business."

"It's fine, Mom." Heath knew his brother wouldn't know Ally. She lived in a whole different world from Jackson's life surrounded by the rich and famous. Hell, didn't they all?

"She works at the hospital."

Jackson nodded. "Is that smart? Isn't there something wrong with dating a woman who works in the same place as you?"

Heath rose to leave. "Says the man who dates the models and actresses he photographs. And actually, no, there's not. I do rounds at the hospital, but it's not like I'm in a position of authority over her. She's a lab tech."

"Cool. But you don't really *date*." Jackson cocked his head to the side and looked at Heath out of the corner of his eye. "She must be a knockout."

Heath leaned down and kissed his mother's cheek. "Have a nice evening, Mom. I'll see you in a few days." He held a hand up for Jackson to smack as he walked by. "See ya, Jackson."

"Should I take that brush-off to mean she's a dog or you're not sharing?"

Heath laughed. "Take it however you want. Oh, and, Jackson, I talked to Brett Bad today. He said to tell you that he'd do the calendar, whatever that means."

Jackson did a fist pump. "Coop and I were hired to shoot next years' charity calendar, featuring the hottest models and local firemen. I thought Brett would want to be one of the firemen. What did you call him for?"

"He hooked me up with the guy who runs the Central Park Zoo. For my date."

"You're taking your date to a zoo? No wonder you don't date often. Hey, I'm meeting Logan and Coop Thursday night for drinks at NightCaps. Join us?"

"Sure."

As Heath walked out, he could hear his mother telling Jackson that *he* should be so lucky as to find a nice girl to go out with.

He texted Ally before driving home.

Running a little late. He looked at his watch and cringed. He was supposed to pick her up at six thirty and it was already six twenty. He was running more than a little late. *I need to run home and shower. Is seven thirty okay?* He deleted the text and called instead, fully expecting her to give him shit for messing up their first real date.

"Hello, Dr. Wild."

He heard a smile in her voice, and it did funny things to his stomach.

"Hi, Ally. I'm really sorry, but I'm running late. Would you mind if I picked you up at seven thirty?"

"No, not at all. I stopped at the library on my way home, so I'm running a little late, too."

The library. He wondered what type of books she liked to read. Another thought that was so strange it opened his eyes to how she was getting under his skin.

"Great. I'm just going to run home and shower. I'll be there shortly."

"Sounds good, *wild boy*."

The way she said *wild boy*, full of innuendo, made his body ache with desire.

"Everything you do and say kills me."

"Kills you in a good way or a bad way?" she asked with a raspy voice.

"In a *very* good way," Heath answered. "You'd better be careful or I'm going to stop behaving myself and we'll both need a cold shower before we even go out."

He spent the next forty minutes wondering how he was going to make it through the night without tearing her clothes off.

Chapter Seven

"LET ME GET this straight. You have no idea where he's taking you or anything? Just that he's a doctor. Dr. Heath Wild. I'm Googling him now," Mandy said.

"Would you stop? Please?"

"You're my sister. I have to make sure this—oh. Hey, sis, he's noted as one of the best sports medicine ortho docs in the city."

"He is? Wait, don't tell me anything else." Ally paced, holding Fifi in one hand and the phone in the other. "I don't want anything like that in my head. It's better if I just think of him as Heath, the guy I met at the conference."

Amanda sighed. "Right. Otherwise you'll go into your I-don't-fit-into-his-world crap. Ally, you work in the hospital. Do I have to remind you again about how pretty and smart you are?"

"It's not that. It's just, you know I work with a lot of not-so-nice docs, and even though Marty rated him a one—"

"He did? Good. I trust Marty. I liked him from the first time you introduced us. He's a straight shooter."

"You met him once," Ally reminded her.

"Yes, but I really liked him. If he says he's a one, he probably is. So what's the issue?"

"No issue. I just don't want to fish for information. Let this progress naturally, so I can see if it should or not."

"Okay. You'll text me if you need me? I still can't believe your mystery man asked you out. You have all the luck." Amanda blew a kiss through the phone. "Have fun, and I'll keep my phone on in case you want me to come kick his ass."

Ally laughed. "He's about six three. I don't think you and I together would be able to do much in that regard, but honestly, as animalistic as he is in the bedroom, he seems really kind otherwise. I think."

"You think." Amanda giggled. "That's really good, sis. Maybe you shouldn't end up in bed with him tonight."

"I'm already planning on keeping our convos outside the bedroom."

"Really? Wow. Good for you."

A knock at the door made her heart leap. "I think he's here."

"Have fun, and remember, no bedroom."

She ended the call, wondering if she was strong enough to stick to the no-bedroom idea. She carried Fifi while she answered the door. Her resolve melted at the sight of Heath's broad shoulders filling the doorway, with a bouquet of orange roses in his hands and an easy smile that warmed her all over. The black cotton shirt he wore was stretched tight across his shoulders, and his low-slung jeans fit him perfectly in all the right places. He wore a pair of leather loafers that probably cost more than her monthly rent, and when he leaned in close to kiss her cheek, he smelled different, woodsier than he had earlier.

"Hey there, beautiful." He handed her the flowers. "These are for you."

Oh, that voice. It made her insides flutter every time she heard him speak.

"Hi. Come in." She stepped aside so he could come into her apartment. Her nerves flared for a brief moment over what he'd think of her cozy home.

"Thank you." She looked down at Fifi.

"May I?" He reached for the kitty and nuzzled her against his chin, then kissed the top of her head. "She's adorable. You must hate to leave her every day."

Ally filled a vase with water and tried to ignore the way he was making her heart go pitter-patter. She eyed him skeptically. "You're either really good at knowing what to say to seduce a woman, or you're a very special man." *Or both.*

He joined her in the kitchen with Fifi cuddled along one thick arm, purring loudly.

"I think we already know that I can sweet-talk *you* into bed, and no one else matters." He tucked Ally's long hair behind her ear and leaned his shoulder against the fridge, then kissed Fifi's head again. "I don't need to use animals for props. I really do love them."

Ally pressed her hand to his chest and breathed deeply. She liked the way his muscles jumped beneath her palms and his eyes narrowed slightly when she touched him.

"What are tonight's rules?"

He wrinkled his brow. "Rules?"

"Well, when we met it was no last names, no particulars. Now you know where I work and where I live. What's next?" She took Fifi and laid her in her bed by the couch.

Heath wrapped his arms around Ally from behind and kissed her neck. "I don't need any more rules, Allyson. Dating is sort of new territory for me." He turned her in his arms and ran his knuckle down her cheek. "Do you want rules?"

She thought about that for a moment before answering. Did

she want to put restraints on their relationship, or would rules make sex even more appealing for both of them?

"Allyson, what is going on in that brilliant mind of yours?" He kissed her forehead, and she smiled up at him.

"I have no idea. Part of me thinks we should try to go on a date without ending up in bed, but the other part of me thinks that will make me want you even more." Where was this honesty coming from?

He tightened his hold on her waist. "All I can say is that this scares the shit out of me, too."

"Is that what I was saying?" She wrinkled her brow, knowing he'd hit the nail on the head.

THE FIRST THING that struck Ally was the way their hands fit together as they walked toward the restaurant. She'd felt Heath's hands in and on her body, but holding his hand was an experience all its own. His hands were thick and strong, yet soft and warm. Just as he carried himself with confidence, his grip was sure and safe. It was a nice feeling. She'd never paid much attention to things like how hands fit together before, but with Heath, she felt acutely aware of every little thing about him. When they stopped to let someone pass in front of them, he tightened his grip on her hand, and when he held the restaurant door open for her, his hand slid to her lower back in a possessive touch she thoroughly enjoyed.

They were asked to leave their shoes at the door of the restaurant. Ally had never been to Hangawi, though she'd heard of the Korean vegetarian restaurant. It was an interesting choice for a first date. The tables were low to the ground, and there wasn't a chair in sight. They sat on pillows on the floor, and instead of sitting across from her, Heath sat beside her. The first hour of their first date was already ten times more intimate than any date she'd ever been on.

"I hope this is okay." Heath reached for her hand.

"Perfect. I've never been here, and I've been curious about it."

"I haven't been here before either, but I figured if I was stepping out of my comfort zone, I might as well go all the way." The side of his mouth quirked up. "No pun intended." He leaned forward and kissed her like it was the most natural thing in the world. Other than her racing heart, it was.

"Out of your comfort zone? What do you mean?"

His eyes went serious, and he took a drink before answering. "Ally, I work hard and my life is complicated. I have familial obligations that I take seriously, and because of those things, I've just never bothered with dating."

"'Familial obligations'? Like, divorced with a child or two? Or…married?" She held her breath while she waited for him to answer. She was not going to get involved with a married man.

He shook his head and brushed her hair from her shoulder. "You do this cute thing when you're worried. You draw your brows together and nibble on your lower lip."

"Way to avoid the question." She readied herself to leave. "If you're married, I don't want—"

"Ally, I'm not married. I told you I don't lie, and cheating is lying. I spend a lot of time with my family. My mother and brothers. It's complicated."

"Oh, sorry. I thought…Complicated how?"

He pressed his lips to the point where her brows drew to-gether. "Sorry. Sidetracked."

She smiled. *He* was complicated. He was a fierce lover, but he was revealing a gentler side that she wanted to get to know better.

"My mother is blind, and my brothers and I take turns going over to spend time with her, take her on errands, out to dinner, you know, things like that."

She reached for his hand, feeling all of her muscles go soft. "That's so sweet of you, but how is that complicated?"

"It's just busy. We have dinner there Sunday nights, too, and that time with my family is important to me. Between my work schedule and my family, I don't have much time for doting on someone."

"I think it's wonderful that you cherish the time you have with your family and you're dedicated to your patients, but did you really just use the word 'doting'?" She smiled.

"What's wrong with 'doting'?" His eyes went serious again.

"Nothing." She laughed. "It's not something guys usually say." She leaned in close and whispered, "Especially guys who talk dirty."

"Well, see? I *am* complicated." He leaned in even closer and said, "And I'd like to dote on you in several dirty ways." He kissed her cheek as the waiter brought their food.

They shared their meals, and conversation came easily. Ally noticed that she was the focus of Heath's attention throughout the meal, despite the attractive women seated at what seemed like every other table. After he paid for their meal, he hailed a cab and they headed for a *secret* destination.

"Tell me about your family, Ally. Are you from New York?"

"I'm supposed to think and speak coherently when you've told me you're whisking me off to a *secret* destination?"

He shrugged. "Testing your ability to multitask."

"I like you, Heath Wild." She drew in a deep breath.

"The feeling's mutual." He touched her chin.

While her insides did a happy dance, she answered his question. "I grew up just outside of the city, where my parents still live. I want to SUNY Cortland. It was cheap, so it wasn't a hardship on my parents, and my sister had gone there, so it felt safe."

"You have a sister?"

"Yes. Amanda. *Mandy*. She's a year older than me. We're really close. In fact, she lives around the corner from me and works near the hospital as a paralegal."

"That's nice. How often do you see your folks?" he asked as the cab pulled over in front of the Central Park Zoo.

"Um. Heath? You know the zoo is closed, right?"

He paid the cabdriver and came around to open her door. "It's closed to the public, yes. But I pulled a few strings. Talk to me, Ally. Tell me about your folks as we walk."

He took her hand and guided her around the main gate. He was taking her to the zoo? At night? This was so romantic that she was having a hard time keeping her focus.

"My parents?"

"Your parents," he urged.

"My dad is an accountant, and my mom stayed home with us when we were little, but now she works part-time at the library and volunteers just about everywhere she can."

Heath led her to a gate where a tall blond man who looked to be in his late thirties was waiting for them.

"Heath, good to see you again." The man shook Heath's hand and smiled at Ally. He had a friendly smile, the kind that said he clearly understood that this was a special evening for them. "You must be Allyson. I'm George. Nice to meet you."

"Hi, George. Nice to meet you, too."

They followed George into the zoo, and he locked the gate behind them. "Okay, guys, enjoy. I'll be waiting here when you're done." He pointed to a bench where a pregnant blond woman was sitting. Heath waved, and the woman waved back as Heath guided Ally in the opposite direction.

"That's his wife, Julie," Heath explained.

"He's just going to let us wander around? What if we do something bad, like jump into an animal's enclosure?" They walked along the wide path toward the animal habitats.

Heath laughed. "I think he trusts my judgment. Should I trust yours?"

He draped an arm over her shoulder and pulled her against him. Moonlight cast a hazy glow over the pavement. "You said you'd never been to a zoo. I thought it was something we could do that was different."

"This is different, all right." She stopped walking and touched his chest again. "This is so special. Thank you, but you didn't have to go to all this trouble."

"Well, don't get too excited yet. We may not see any animals this late at night."

"I don't care if we don't see any animals. It was such a thoughtful thing to arrange. Thank you, Heath." She went up on her toes, and he met her halfway in a sweet kiss. His lips were warm and moist, inviting. As he deepened the kiss, her body melted against him, and she didn't want the kiss to end. His hands splayed against her back, and she could feel his strength through his chest, his biceps, his thighs pressing against hers. When their lips finally parted, she was breathless for more.

"I sure like you, Allyson," he said softly.

"Ditto," was all she could manage.

As they neared the animal habitats, musky scents hung in the air. Without the road noises or people milling about, Ally was focused on Heath. His stride felt easier, as if he wasn't on alert, ready to fend off strangers, like he seemed to be when they were out on the busy streets. Ally thought they'd hear animal noises more clearly at night, but there weren't many discernible animal sounds, just the sounds of their shoes on the pavement and every now and again a random feral noise in the distance.

They walked through the aviary, and she was delighted to hear the sounds of wings flapping, as they must have scared a bird into flight. Ally's sense of smell and sound were heightened, but while she tried to focus on spotting birds, she was distracted by the man standing beside her and the feel of his shoulder pressing intimately against hers.

Heath was right: They didn't see many animals, but just being together was nice, walking in the moonlight, having the zoo all to themselves. Knowing that he cared enough to go to the trouble of pulling whatever strings it took for him to get George to open the zoo made Ally feel special.

She marveled at the way her heart skipped a beat when the glowing eyes of deer appeared in the tufted deer habitat. Deer were fairly common. Why did this feel so magical? Heath kissed her temple, and she had her answer. Being with Heath was magical. Everything else—the animal sightings and sounds—was a gift.

As they made their way through the zoo, the otter and porcupines were not curious enough to appear when they passed. They continued along the path, and Ally felt like every minute brought her and Heath closer together. She glanced at him, and he smiled down at her. Each time he caught her sneaking glances, he pulled her in closer, and she felt as though they were becoming more than just physically close. They were both relaxing into their surprise coupling.

"You were cute in the lab today," Heath said as they walked around the temperate territory, where the snow monkeys and red pandas were kept.

"Cute? I was so nervous. I had no idea you worked there."

They stopped at the stone wall by the snow monkeys, and he tugged her in close again. "Nervous? What worried you?"

"Well, let's see. You and I were both looking for a night of no-strings-attached fun, which somehow turned into two nights, and *then* you somehow got me to have phone sex with you. Then you top it off by walking into the lab where I work. What about all of that sounds comfortable to you? I wasn't sure if you'd be pissed that I worked there, or, for that matter, if *I* would be that *you* worked there. I was kind of shocked, to be honest. I had just written you off."

"Written me off? Why?" He tightened his grip on her hips. "Am I that bad?"

"No, but..." Her eyes skated nervously over the monkey enclosure. Rocks lined a pool of water moving in the evening breeze on the far side of the exhibit. Ally tried to figure out how to explain what she'd felt earlier.

He stepped into her line of sight and gazed into her eyes with a soft, worried look that she hadn't seen before.

"Talk to me, Ally. We've both been lied to. We established that the other night. I'm not going to do that to you."

"I'm not worried about that." She dropped her gaze. "Or maybe I am. I'm not sure. But this afternoon I realized I was anxiously awaiting each text from you, and I kept thinking, what happens when they stop? Eventually they would, and I'd already felt myself getting tied up in you in a way that I probably shouldn't."

"That's why we're here." He said it so easily, like it made perfect sense, and she didn't have a clue what he meant.

"At the zoo?"

"No, sweetheart." He smiled again.

Somehow his words, his smile, eased her worries. He looked trustworthy and sincere, and she knew it was genuine, but she'd been hurt before.

Hasn't everyone?

She hated the conflicting feelings warring inside her.

"That's why we're on this date," he explained. "I was feeling the same things, Ally. I've never checked my cell phone as many times as I have in the last two days. I couldn't stop thinking about you. I had to find out why, and when I saw you in the lab, all my rules about dating came crashing down."

HEATH COULDN'T BELIEVE the words that were spewing from his mouth. They were all true, but he hadn't realized how strongly he'd felt them. He could tell by the worry in Ally's eyes that she was struggling with this as much as he was, and all he wanted was to make her worries go away.

That wasn't exactly true.

He wanted much more.

"But why, Heath? Why are we feeling this way after the things we did?"

"What do you mean? If you have great sex, it can't lead to something more?" Didn't most women want something more? Now he was flat-out confused. "I have to be honest. I have been confused as hell over all of this, but then I thought, why fight it?"

She touched her forehead to his chest, and he held her close. There beneath the moon and the stars, outside the snow monkey enclosure in Central Park, Heath felt his world shift and his heart open.

He cupped her face between his hands and tilted it toward his, searching her eyes for answers. He didn't even know what the questions were, but somehow he knew that whatever the answers were, they lay within her.

"We'll go slow, Ally."

He was rewarded with another sweet smile. He couldn't help but press his lips to hers.

"We can start by you telling me your last name."

She laughed, and it was music to his ears. "Jenner. Allyson Jenner."

"Related to Bruce?"

She shook her head, and he lowered his lips to hers again. "You really are the most intriguing woman I know, Allyson Jenner."

They left the zoo a short while later, having seen few animals and discovering a whole new world within each other.

They walked back to Ally's apartment, and by the time they reached her door, Heath didn't want the night to end. He couldn't remember the last time he'd enjoyed spending time with a woman so much or hadn't wished he was reading a medical journal or catching up on sports instead. When he was with Ally, the rest of the world fell away.

"Do you want to come in for a drink?" she offered.

It was nearly midnight, and Heath knew she had to get up early, as did he, but when she blinked up at him with her big doe eyes, he couldn't resist accepting.

"Sure."

She unlocked the door, and the first thing she did when she walked inside was bend down to pick up Fifi and give her a snuggle. He wondered if she was nervous, or if she was overly comfortable. He found that *he* was both. He was overly comfortable with Ally *and* he was nervous about where to take things from here.

Her efficiency apartment smelled like spring, fresh and floral. To the right was a small kitchen counter and a row of three cabinets, with a breakfast bar and two black stools tucked beneath it. Scarred hardwood floors and white walls gave the small space an airy feel. Heath's eyes rolled over the simple sofa and television and moved to the king-sized bed just beyond.

"Wine okay?" she asked as she reached for two glasses.

"Yeah, sure." He picked up Fifi and petted her while he discovered more about Ally. "I like your apartment."

She looked around the room. "The efficiency makes it easier for Fifi to navigate. The fewer walls the better."

That made sense. He thought about his mother and the way she trailed her fingers along the walls of the home she refused to give up. He was sure she knew every squeaky floorboard, every nook and cranny on each floor. He lifted Fifi and kissed her head as he eyed Ally. It took a special person to care for a blind pet, and as he watched Ally put fresh water into the cat's bowl before pouring their wine, he knew she was the perfect person for Fifi. The question was, was she the perfect person for him, too?

On the coffee table he found her library books—all medical, which surprised him. He picked one up and waved it in Ally's direction.

"So the lab is more than just a place to work for you?"

She shrugged as she joined him by the sofa and handed him a glass of wine. She sipped her wine, and Heath wondered how anyone could make skinny jeans and a turquoise blouse look sexy as hell.

He set Fifi in her bed as they sank down to the couch beside each other.

"There was a time when I thought I wanted to go to medical school, but I didn't have the money, and I'm not sure I really wanted it enough to succeed. So, when something medical catches my eye, I read up on it. It's really just hit or miss. A weird hobby, I guess." She flipped through a book about human anatomy and physiology. "What I really like is the patient interaction and figuring out the puzzles. Fact finding, I guess. The ability to find definitive, or close to definitive, answers."

"The lab work." There were very distinct people in medicine, those who belonged behind the scenes and those who belonged with the patients. And Ally was definitely not a behind-the-scenes woman. She had a warm, charming personality, and he imagined she would have made a wonderful doctor.

"Yes, but I love the patient contact, too. Right now the position at the hospital fulfills both of those sides of my personality. It's a good match."

He took the book from her lap and set it and his wineglass on the table, then sat back, facing Ally with one arm across the back of the sofa. She set her wineglass next to his and relaxed beside him.

"You said you volunteered at the conference. Why?"

"If I volunteer, I get to take home transcripts of the lectures and discussions. I know that makes me nerdy, but I like it. It's like Christmas several times a year."

"So, it's not the trip itself, or access to all the docs…"

She narrowed her eyes, and he held her gaze. "You think I went to hook up with doctors?"

"I wasn't thinking that, but I'd be lying if I said it hadn't crossed my mind. Considering the way we met, didn't it cross yours that I might go to conferences to hook up with women?"

She lowered her eyes and traced the seam of her jeans with her finger. "Yes, but I've been trying not to think about it."

He lifted her chin and pressed his lips softly to hers. "I'm an honest guy, and tonight I feel closer to you than I've felt to a woman in years. I want to keep seeing you, and I don't want any secrets. I won't judge you, and I hope that you won't judge me either, but I know that's a lot to ask."

She searched his eyes, and he wondered what she was thinking. Would she be as honest with him as he planned to be with her? Would his propensity for semi-anonymous flings be the end of their relationship? More importantly, would he be able to handle her truth—whatever that might be?

"Are you sure you want to go there?" She nervously twisted a lock of her hair. "I mean, you might not like what you hear, and I know I'm not going to like what you tell me."

"I think you just gave me indication enough of your answer, and you're right. I might not like hearing it, but we can't build a relationship on ignoring the past."

She met his gaze. "So you want to do this? You want to date and see where we end up? Even though we both work at the hospital? Even though I'm a lab tech and you're a doctor? That doesn't bother you?"

"Allyson, do I act like the kind of guy who's hung up on status?"

"No. But you have things you need to ask, and so do I."

He smiled, because she was not a pushover, and he could see that her strength would push him in ways he wasn't used to—and probably needed.

"Fair enough. I love that you are doing something that fulfills you. That's all anyone can hope for in their lifetime. My mother was a seamstress, and my father worked in a factory, and I cannot remember them ever being unhappy. They had time for me and my brothers, and they had time for each other. The way I see it, if you decide to sell flowers on the street corner because that makes you happy, then that's your prerogative. The same way that if I decide tomorrow, or in ten years, that I am sick of being a doctor and want to sell shoes for a living, I'd expect you to accept me in the same way you do now."

She scooted closer to him and placed her hand on his arm on the back of the couch, and the combination of her sincere smile and that gentle touch solidified in Heath's mind that he wanted to share these secrets, no matter how painful it might be.

"You sure you can handle this?" she asked.

"No, but I want to try. You?"

"Same. But you go first, because if I can't handle what you tell me, then there's no need to embarrass myself." She drew in a deep breath and pulled her shoulders back. "Okay, go. But I have a feeling this isn't going to be a quick sting like giving blood. So just say it quickly." She clenched her jaw, and he had to touch it. He reached out and stroked her cheek.

"You sure?"

She nodded, and he had the urge to hold her close to keep her from walking away. Instead, he simply did as she asked and hoped for the best.

"The way we met. The no-personal-information, first-name-only sex. That's pretty much the guy I've been for the last few years. No ties. Literally and figuratively." He paused, letting the truth sink in. She pressed her lips together but didn't say anything, so he continued speaking in a gentle tone, hating the acidic taste of the man he'd been. "I don't go to conferences for that purpose, obviously, but if someone interests me...And around here? In the city? I don't really date, and I never have flings. I have a few women I get together with on and off, but it's a mutually agreed upon arrangement. We don't date. We're—"

"Friends with benefits?" She raised her brows.

He shook his head. "Not even that. We're fuck buddies."

She nodded and dropped her eyes, twisting another lock of hair.

"And if we continue to go out?" she asked tentatively.

"All that stops." The words left his mouth with confidence, though they shocked him. He scrubbed his hand down his face and repeated them more for himself than for her. "All that stops."

Ally was silent for what felt like several minutes, though it was probably only a few seconds. "Okay, well. Wait." Her eyes bloomed wide. "You said *literally* about no ties. What does that mean?"

"It means that what we did I don't usually do. I have, years ago, in college, with a girl I dated for two years, but not since." His chest constricted with the realization of what that meant. He must have seen something in Ally from the start that made him feel comfortable enough to go there with her. "Holy...I didn't even realize that."

"The girl who cheated?"

He nodded.

"Were you in love with her?" There was no hint of jealousy in her voice, but her eyes warmed with compassion.

He lifted one shoulder in a shrug. "I thought I was. But I don't know."

Her brows knitted together. "I'm sorry. That must have been a very painful experience."

"It was, and it's not one that I've shared with many people, which makes me wonder what exactly you've done to me, Allyson Jenner."

To his surprise, she crawled over his lap and straddled him, pressing her hands to his shoulders and flashing a playful smile.

"I don't know, but I'm going to keep you pinned here while I tell you about myself, because guys are weird when it comes to women." She ran her finger along the collar of his T-shirt. "That whole double standard thing sort of freaks me out. So this way you have to at least hear me out before walking out of this apartment."

"You do realize you're totally turning me on right now, right?" He lifted his hips and caught her lower lip between his teeth before pressing a kiss to it.

"Yes, well, that's the danger of pinning a man beneath you, I suppose."

"Allyson, are you sure you're okay with what I've told you?"

A serious expression slid over her face. "You're not a teenager, Heath. If you weren't sexually active, I'd think it was a little weird. If I were my sister, I might have ended things right away. Mandy's great, but she doesn't see sex the same way I do."

"And how is that?" He fingered the ends of her hair.

"I'm not sure how to put it into words without it sounding bad, but it's kind of a stress reliever or a rejuvenator. Gosh, that makes me sound slutty." She started to slide off his lap. He settled his hands on her hips and held her in place.

"Stay. Talk to me."

"I...I haven't had many sexual partners, but I've had a handful." She searched his eyes, and he knew she was looking for his response. He wasn't ready to form one yet. He wanted to hear what else she had to say.

"And?" he urged.

"I haven't dated anyone seriously since my last boyfriend cheated." She narrowed her eyes and pointed a finger at Heath. "Before I say any more..." She dropped her finger and softened her tone. "I'm realizing how stupid it is to think that a no-strings-attached guy might be faithful when other guys who *asked* for monogamy couldn't."

"You do realize that being faithful comes from within, right? I made a decision not to be in a monogamous relationship because I'd been hurt and didn't want to experience that again, not because I cheated."

"Me too." She twisted her hair again. "Are we fooling ourselves?"

"That depends. Are *you* a cheater? Because I *know* I'm *not*."

"No, I'm not a cheater!" She swatted his chest.

"Then we're not fooling ourselves."

"So, you can handle my promiscuous past?"

He saw the worry in her eyes. "Sweetheart, you weren't exactly sleeping around with half the docs in the hospital." He arched a brow and she smiled. "As long as from now on there's only me, I think I can handle it."

He lowered her to the couch and came down over her smiling face. "Besides, I really..." He kissed her lips. "Really." He kissed her jaw. "Really like you."

"I have one more question."

"Mm-hmm?" He nibbled on her neck.

"Have you...? It's hard to concentrate with you doing that." She closed her eyes and rested her head back.

"Finish your thought," he whispered against her ear, before taking her lobe into his mouth and making her brain fuzzy again.

"Safe sex." She panted. "Have you always practiced safe sex?"

He drew back, knowing he was looking at her like she was ridiculous, but he couldn't stop himself. "Yes. You?"

"Always." She pulled him into a hard, fast kiss. "Now please show me how much you want this to work between us before it's time to get ready for work again."

Chapter Eight

"I CAN'T BELIEVE you are working on three hours of sleep," Amanda said as they carried their lunch trays to a table in the crowded hospital cafeteria Tuesday afternoon. "And you still manage to look as pretty as Rachel Bilson. So not fair." Amanda and Ally looked similar in body type and hair color, but Amanda wore her hair straight and shoulder length while Ally wore hers longer and let her natural waves tumble freely. The other big difference was that Amanda dressed in a preppy style while Ally tended to dress trendier, sexier.

Ally sank into a chair with a sigh. "Good sex is rejuvenating. How many times have I told you that? And Rachel Bilson? She looks twelve. Can't I be a young Sandra Bullock? She looks smarter and has a *real* body."

"Fine, Sandra it is." Amanda speared her salad with her fork and pointed it like a loaded gun at Ally. "You're sure about this guy, right? You think you can trust him?"

"You're asking if I can trust a guy I made out with the first time I met him. I had to trust him then, or I would have been opening myself up to something really dangerous."

"Well," Amanda said as she chewed her lunch. "I would never do what you did. Just sayin'."

"Whatever. No judging. Besides, we've both been on the other side of the hurt mobile. I think we're actually well suited for each other." Her mind traveled back to the evening before and the amazing connection they'd shared. The way their bodies had moved together, the way he'd felt inside her and how she'd hated to see him leave in the wee hours of the morning.

"Did I tell you he brought me orange roses?"

"Yes." Amanda feigned a dreamy sigh. "The color of fiery passion."

They both laughed.

"You're the luckiest girl I know," Amanda said.

"In this case, I think I'd agree."

"Can you still go out with me Thursday night, or will you blow me off now that you have a boyfriend?"

Ally's fork stopped midair. "Say that again."

"Can you still—"

"No, the last part."

Amanda scrunched her face. "Now that you have a boyfriend?"

"I like the sound of that. Do you know how long I've *not* wanted a boyfriend?" She felt herself smiling as she met her sister's gaze.

"Since Chet, so that would be, what? Nine months?" Amanda shook her head.

"Exactly. Doesn't that tell you something? Because it tells me something loud and clear. I wasn't looking for a boyfriend. So this must be right. It feels right."

"For your sake, I hope so, sis. Just be careful, you know?" Amanda looked around the cafeteria, then leaned across the table and whispered, "You work here. What if people find out?" She lifted her eyes over Ally's shoulder, and as Ally felt a familiar, heavy hand grip her shoulder, Amanda's eyes widened and her jaw dropped open.

Heath came around Ally's side and smiled down at her. "Hi, Ally. I don't want to interrupt, but I thought I'd say hi. I was doing rounds and needed a little pick-me-up." He held up a coffee cup as his eyes flicked to Amanda. "Hi. I'm Heath."

He held out a hand, and Amanda shook it, blinking off her stupor while Ally tried to calm her racing heart. Heath looked delicious in a pair of dark slacks and a light blue dress shirt with a striped silk tie. Oh, what she'd like to do with that tie. She felt her cheeks heat up and was thankful when Amanda's introduction distracted her from her dirty thoughts.

"Hi. I'm Amanda, Ally's sister."

"I thought I noticed a resemblance. Hi, Amanda. It's a pleasure to meet you." Heath touched Ally's cheek, and she met his gaze. "Are you free after work? There's someplace I'd like to show you."

"Sure. I work until five."

"I'm afraid I have to work later. Can I pick you up around seven?"

"That sounds perfect." He squeezed her hand and said goodbye.

As he walked away, Ally released a breath she hadn't realized she'd been holding.

"Whoa, you are taken with him." Amanda nudged Ally's shoulder. "And now I see why. He's really hot."

"That he is." Ally tried to act like her stomach wasn't doing flips, when it was all she could do to remain seated and not run around like a lovesick woman with a silly grin on her face and say, *He's mine! That magnificent man is mine!*

"Al, he looked at you like Dad looks at Mom."

Their parents had been high school sweethearts, and to this day, they still looked at each other like they were the only ones in the room. To find that type of love was more than Ally could imagine. Now her sister's comment had her reassessing the intensity that she saw in Heath's eyes every time he looked at her. Could Amanda be right?

She chewed on that thought all afternoon. By the time Heath knocked on Ally's door that evening, they'd already shared several screens' worth of sexy texts, and she couldn't wait to be in his arms again.

"Hi," she said as she pulled the door open.

With one strong arm Heath swept her body to his and claimed her mouth in a hungry, demanding kiss.

"I missed you," he said against her lips before kissing her again. The kiss was slow and so intense that she felt her insides shatter with desire.

She twined her arms around his neck and kissed him more urgently, moaning as he reciprocated and lifted her into his arms. Her legs circled his waist, and his hands slid beneath her skirt and immediately into her panties, furtively seeking her pleasure. She'd never wanted a man so completely, craved him so intensely that she would give herself up in the first few minutes of coming together—and with Heath, she couldn't get enough of him, or give herself up fast enough.

"Oh, baby," he said into her mouth. He drew back, and his eyes were dark with desire. "You're so wet."

"I've been thinking about you all day." She lowered her lips to his. "Those texts. God, Heath. I never knew I could get so turned on just thinking about you being hard."

He slid his fingers inside her, and her head tipped back. "Yes."

He carried her across the floor toward the bed.

"I had such a nice date planned." He kissed her again, all

the while driving her crazy with his fingers, teasing, taunting, making her insides swell with need.

"Later," she whispered.

He lowered her down to the bed on her back, and she slid to the edge and reached for the button of his pants as he loosened his tie and took off his shirt.

"Keep your tie," she said as she fumbled with his button and zipper, then yanked down his slacks and briefs, freeing his eager erection.

She looked up as she wrapped her fingers around his hard length.

"I should text you more often," he teased.

She dragged her tongue from base to tip, and he sucked in air between gritted teeth, fisting his hands in her hair as she took him in her mouth. She cradled his balls with one hand while stroking him with the other, sucking and licking until he was breathing hard, guiding her efforts with not-so gentle tugs of her hair that heightened her arousal.

"Lie down on your back," she said as she wiggled out of her clothes.

Ally had never seen anything as appealing as Heath Wild lying naked on her bed, stroking his erection while watching her strip.

She grabbed his tie from where he'd set it on the bedside table and straddled him.

His eyes narrowed. "Ally?"

She lifted his hand and sucked his fingers into her mouth. Her taste still lingered on his skin. She knew that would turn him on *and* distract him from what she wanted to do.

"Christ, Ally," he whispered as she began wrapping the silk around his thick wrist.

She felt his muscles tense.

"Ally." A warning.

"What?"

"I've never been on this end of things."

That stopped her cold—and excited the hell out of her. She leaned over him and traced his lips with her tongue.

"Then I'll be your first. I like that."

"Ally. I don't know." His chest heaved beneath her with each heavy breath.

"Don't you trust me?"

"Explicitly." Truth rang in his voice and in his eyes.

She pressed her lips to his. "Then let me explore. If you hate it, I'll stop."

One quick nod was all the approval she needed. She bound his wrists and tied the ends to the decorative white iron slats on her headboard, and then she pressed her hands to his chest and followed her fingers over his pecs with her mouth. She flicked his nipples with her tongue, teasing them into hard peaks, then lowered her mouth over one, sucking gently as his hips rose off the bed.

"Holly fuck. You're…Ally."

She lifted her eyes, still teasing his nipple.

"Fuck. Fuck, Ally."

She smiled around her tongue, then traveled lower, tasting every inch of his incredible abdominal muscles, to the rounded arch of his thigh. She sucked the inside of one powerful thigh as she stroked his cock. Then she blew over the wet spot and nudged his legs open wider with her knees.

"Ally," he whispered in one heated breath.

She licked his balls, feeling them tighten against her tongue, then licked the glistening slit at the tip of his arousal.

"Ally," he whispered. "Christ, Ally." His eyes opened and blazed through her. "Suck me, baby."

Hearing those words from his mouth made her wetter. She moved up the bed, ravishing his mouth as her nimble fingers quickly untied his bindings. He growled into her mouth as he sat up and tried to move her beneath him.

"No. I'm not done." She loved seeing him reclining in her bed, with all his glorious planes of flesh and muscle taut and ready for her. She loved the control of being on top and the empowering feeling of knowing he'd been bound. She wasn't ready to relinquish control just yet.

She licked her palm.

"Fuck," he whispered as she stroked his erection. "Fuck. Ally, you're going to make me come."

"When I'm ready I will," she teased, and turned around on her hands and knees.

She straddled his chest and lowered her mouth over his cock as he gripped her hips and lowered her wetness to his mouth. His talented tongue moved in and out, over and around her swollen, needy flesh as she stroked and sucked his hard length. He slid his fingers inside her, and she arched back with a sigh.

"Oh my, that feels good." She closed her eyes, reveling in the feel of his fingers fucking her while his tongue stroked her clit.

"Suck me," he said. Then his mouth returned to her with renewed energy.

"Heath. Don't stop."

She swallowed him deep and sucked hard as his fingers drove in and out of her. She quickened her efforts as her climax built. Her focus ebbed and flowed as waves of desire surged through her. Their bodies were covered in a sheen of sweat. The sounds of skin against skin and moans filled the air. Her legs tingled and her belly grew hot as lust coiled deep inside her. Just as her muscles tightened around his fingers, she felt his cock swell in her hands, and he came in hot, salty spurts down her throat as her own intense orgasm tore through her. She continued sucking, swallowing all he had to give as her muscles contracted and ripples of ecstasy rolled through her.

He gathered her trembling, weak body in his arms and kissed her with warmth and tenderness. Neither of them flinched at the taste of themselves on the other's mouth. None of that mattered. Ally was lost in the sensual aftermath of their lovemaking.

Chapter Nine

TWO HOURS LATER, after Heath had run a warm bath for them and they'd lingered in it until their skin pruned, they'd dressed and ordered Chinese food. Now it was after eleven o'clock and they were sitting on the couch. Health held Fifi in his lap while Ally snuggled beneath his arm. He'd never felt more content in his life. It had been years since Heath had stuck around after having sex with a woman, and with Ally he never wanted to leave.

"I'm sorry we missed our date," Ally said as she petted Fifi.

"I'm not." He kissed her temple and hugged her closer. "You're dangerous, Ally."

"Why?" She gazed up at him with innocent eyes.

"Because I never thought I'd meet anyone who…" He paused, realizing that he was about to expose a big part of himself.

"Who?"

He thought about Logan and how quickly he'd fallen for Stormy, and he thought about his parents, who had met and married in the span of seven months. Was it really so crazy to feel himself falling for a woman this fast? Was it just their amazing sexual connection? He gazed into her eyes and knew beyond a shadow of a doubt that it was far more than just the sex. With Ally he felt something deeper than ever before. More all-consuming and intense.

"I never knew I could feel like this," he explained. "That we could connect on so many levels, so fast. We've only known each other a few days, and I don't want to leave you and go back to my place. I want to scoop you and Fifi up and take you with me. I want to wake up next to you tomorrow and shower with you and walk out the front door with you when I go to work. It's crazy."

Ally silently petted Fifi's head. "Where were we going to go on our date tonight?"

His heart sank. She was changing the subject, which could only mean that she wasn't in the same place as he was. She didn't feel what he felt. Rather than answering her question, he asked for the answer he needed.

"Did that freak you out?"

She shook her head, but he felt her muscles tighten, and the inch of space she'd put between them spoke volumes.

"I shouldn't have said anything," Heath said, though in his heart he knew he couldn't have held it back if he'd wanted to.

"It's not that." She turned so she was facing him and stroked his cheek. "You have the most striking jawline."

He narrowed his eyes. "Are you trying to distract me from what I said?"

She shook her head again. "No. I just said what I was thinking, and you didn't freak me out."

"No? Ally, you keep changing the subject. If this is too much too fast…"

"No. I'm a little afraid of what I feel when I'm with you. I'm doing things with you that I haven't done with anyone before, and it all feels so right. But I'm also opening myself up to you so fast. It scares me. My exes cheated after *months* of being together, and I wasn't nearly as close to either of them as I am to you after just a few days."

"What worries you? That we're moving too fast? That I'll cheat? Or that we'll get even closer and *then* I'll cheat?" He pressed his lips to her forehead and pulled her in close again. "Talk to me, Ally."

"You're so communicative," she said with a smile.

"Only with those I choose to be." He'd known last night that he'd do anything for Ally. She was bringing out parts of himself that he hadn't known existed, and now he was beginning to own those parts of himself. It was a new feeling, and while it scared the shit out of him to feel emotions this powerful, the fear of losing what had only just begun scared him even more.

Ally already owned a piece of him that no one else ever had. The thought startled him, but it was another truth he could not deny.

"Tell me what you're afraid of."

"Not that you'll cheat. Guys who cheat are more, I don't know...deceptive, I guess. You're very open. But opening myself up to being hurt, even though I trust you, is scary. It's not like I can stop myself. I don't even *want* to stop myself. Everything with you feels so right, and I know we're moving fast, but I think that's how things are with some people."

"I said we'd go slow, and here I am telling you exactly how I feel. I'm sorry."

A soft laugh carried her smile. "You didn't have to say a word about how you feel. I feel it in your touch, and I see it in your eyes. My sister saw it when she met you."

"Your sister? Was I that transparent today?" His feelings for Ally felt so big that he wasn't surprised to hear her sister had picked up on them.

"She's very intuitive," Ally said, stifling a yawn.

He knew he should leave and let her get some rest, although it was the last thing he wanted to do. He petted Fifi, then brought Ally's hand to his lips, kissed her knuckles, and did the right thing.

"I should let you get some sleep."

She made a whimpering sound and snuggled in closer. He had to fight the urge to carry her to bed and curl up around her.

"You just finished telling me how it scared you to feel so much so fast, and now you're making it hard for me to leave."

She smiled up at him. "I told you I was confused."

He kissed her forehead. "You're adorable when you're confused. Are you busy tomorrow night?"

"No, but I am busy Thursday night."

There was no mistaking the jealousy slithering beneath his skin, which was ridiculous, because he was meeting his brothers Thursday night for drinks, and Ally was free to go out and do whatever she liked.

She ran her finger along the tight line of his lips. "Why is your jaw so tight?"

Because I'm a jealous idiot.

"Is it? Hm." He pressed his lips to hers. "That's better." *Not.*

"Sorry about Thursday. I promised Amanda I'd go out with her."

He breathed a little—a *little*—easier. "That's okay. I'm busy Thursday, too. I'm meeting my brothers for a drink. Tomorrow night, then?"

"Yes."

"It's a date. And I promise not to attack you the minute I walk in the door."

She stuck out her lower lip in a pout. "Aw."

"You are going to be the death of me." He wrapped his arms around her, and when their mouths came together again, he knew if he didn't get up and leave, he never would.

"I should go," he said against her lips.

She pressed her soft hands to his cheeks. "Just one more kiss."

Her mouth covered his hungrily, and he felt himself disappearing into her again, as his hand traveled over the curve of her hip and came to rest on her waist.

"Ally, I'm going to be too hard to walk out of here and you're going to start thinking I only want to be with you for sex. I've got to leave before I carry you to your bed again and make love to you until we're both too tired to get up for work tomorrow." He longed for her to ask him to stay, and the magnitude of that desire hit him square in the chest. For the first time since his college days, he didn't try to deny it or pretend it wasn't consuming his thoughts. To his surprise, he embraced the urge.

"Promises, promises."

He touched his forehead to hers and breathed deeply, wondering how they'd gone from not exchanging last names to not being able to be apart in less than a week.

Chapter Ten

HEATH GOT UP early Wednesday morning, and before he set out for his morning run, he texted Ally.

How can I miss you already?

He ran through Central Park, hoping to quell the jealousy that had prickled his nerves last night and had eaten away at him through the wee hours of the morning. He'd slept fitfully, not because he thought Ally might go behind his back and see another guy, but because after years of not giving a shit about anyone outside of his family—and of course his patients, but that was a different type of caring altogether—he cared, *really cared*, about her. Allyson had gotten under his skin, and he fucking loved it, but he had no idea how to handle the crap that came along with it. How did he shake the feeling of wanting to be with her every minute? And how could he convince her that he would never hurt her the way she'd been hurt before?

More importantly, when had he become clingy?

What the hell was that all about?

The sun was just coming up as he circled back and ran toward home. He spotted his friend Josh Braden, a world-renowned clothing designer, running on the path ahead of him. He and Josh had run together a number of times over the last few years. Heath's father had grown up in Trusty, Colorado, while his mother had grown up in Weston, Colorado, where

Josh's family lived. Heath's parents had been good friends with Hal and Adriana Braden, Josh's parents. Adriana had passed away when the Braden children were young, leaving Hal to raise his six children alone. When Heath was growing up, his parents had sent him and his brothers to work on Hal's ranch for a few weeks each summer. Their father had insisted that hard manual labor instilled morals and a strong sense of self. The weeks they'd spent together had also built a sense of loyalty between the two families.

"Braden!" Heath called as he caught up to Josh.

Josh turned with a ready smile. "Heath, how's it going? I haven't seen you running lately." He was the same height as Heath, with thick dark hair, which was perfectly coiffed even as he ran, dark brown eyes, and a lean, muscular frame.

"I was out of town for a conference, and I've been tied up recently." *Literally.* The thought made him smile. "How's Riley?"

"Great. Getting anxious to have our wedding." Josh and Riley had been engaged, and business partners, for more than a year. They'd both grown up in Weston, but they hadn't started dating until she'd moved to the city to work for Josh.

Heath remembered that Josh and Riley had fallen for each other pretty quickly, too. "Josh, do you mind if I ask you a personal question?"

"Sure. Go ahead."

"How did you know Riley was the right woman for you?"

Josh turned his dark eyes on Heath, and without missing a step he said, "There was never any question. We kissed. I knew." He shifted his eyes to the path ahead of them. "When it's right, you know."

"That simple?"

"How many years have you been running?"

Heath shrugged. "Since high school."

"How did you know you were a runner?" Josh slowed as they came to the entrance of the park.

"One day a buddy asked if I wanted to go for a run. I went, and everything about it felt right. It fed my need to compete, helped clear my head, and gave me more energy than I'd ever had in my life. There was no question *if* I'd run again. It was a matter of how soon I could make it happen."

"And how hard was that?"

"I rearranged my schedule and made time the next day."

Josh cocked his head and smiled. "Exactly. When something's right, nothing can stand in your way. Love's the same."

HEATH SPENT THE afternoon seeing patients and mulling over what Josh had said. There was no doubt in his mind Ally was the only woman he wanted, and hearing Josh say that he'd known in a heartbeat that what he and Riley had was true love, made Heath feel less like his feelings had come *too* fast. They were just fast, and that was okay by him.

He and Ally had exchanged a few sexy texts, and when his phone vibrated in the late afternoon, he was smiling before he even withdrew it from his pocket.

The text was from Logan. He read the message as he walked into his private office, trying to ignore his disappointment.

How's life?

Heath smirked, knowing his brother was fishing for information on Ally. Logan didn't like unanswered questions, and it was probably driving him nuts not being able to uncover everything he could about Ally for Heath.

Damn good. You?

He set his phone on the desk and picked up a patient file to review. Logan's text came in seconds later.

Bringing your new friend to Mom's Sunday?

Heath had been pondering the same thing all day. He hadn't introduced a woman to his family since he was in college. Introducing his family was about the biggest step he could make, second only to spending the night. That was another thing he hadn't done since college, and he wanted to cross that line with Ally. But after their conversation last night, he felt like she'd sent him conflicting messages. She seemed to want to move forward, regardless of how quickly their relationship was progressing, but she'd been honest about it scaring her. Asking her to meet his family might scare her even more—or drive home the realization that he was serious about her.

He reread her text from earlier that morning before returning Logan's text.

Fifi and I were just wondering the same thing. Can't wait to see you tonight. Xo

He smiled as he returned Logan's text.

Maybe.

Heath confirmed that Logan and his brothers still planned to meet tomorrow night at NightCaps. His thoughts drifted back to Ally—not that they ever veered very far from her. He looked around his office, wishing she were there. She'd probably like flipping through his medical journals, which he kept on the bookshelves on the wall by the window. He checked the time and realized he was already late to see his next patient. He picked up the phone and called the front desk.

"Yes, Dr. Wild?"

"Hi, Judy. Would you mind having Katrina put together my archived medical journals and leave them on my desk in a box?" Katrina was a floater, which meant that she helped out in the office wherever she was needed.

He texted Ally on his way to see his next patient. *I have a surprise for you.*

BY WEDNESDAY EVENING Ally could hardly wait to see Heath. She'd texted him a few times after he'd texted to tell her he had a surprise for her, but he hadn't responded. She knew how busy the doctors at the hospital were, and she assumed that Heath's schedule was no different.

After showering and spending way too long picking out an outfit to wear, she loved up Fifi and gave her fresh food and water. Her phone vibrated with a call from Amanda, and she answered it as she crossed the floor to the full-length mirror to check out her outfit one last time.

"Hey, Mandy. What's up?"

"Don't kill me, but I have to break our date for tomorrow night."

She heard a smile in her sister's voice. "No problem. What's so important that you're willing to blow me off?"

"A date!" Amanda squealed into the phone.

Ally pulled the phone away from her ear. "You're going on a date? That's great. With who?"

"He's an attorney. He works in my building."

"Gray suit guy?" Amanda had told her about a hot guy she'd flirted with a number of times in the elevator. She'd referred to him as *gray suit guy*.

"Yes. Are you mad? I know I gave you a hard time about not canceling on me."

"No, of course not. Go, have fun. Cut loose a little and enjoy yourself."

Amanda laughed. "Cut loose? Yeah, okay. I'll inspect his briefs."

Ally laughed at her sister's attempt at legal humor. "My money's on you not inspecting his briefs, but my hope is that you do. It might loosen you up a little."

There was a knock at her door as she ended the call. Ally took one last look in the mirror. Pleased with the midthigh-length navy blue dress she'd chosen, she slipped on her heels and answered the door.

Heath held a giant cardboard box in front of him. He smiled and raked his eyes down her body. "Ally, you look incredible."

"Thank you." She moved to the side so he could come in, and he leaned in for a kiss as he passed.

"You keep dressing like that and we'll really never make it out of here." Heath set the box on the coffee table and reached for her.

She placed her hands on his chest and felt his heartbeat quicken. "I have a feeling that what I wear has very little to do with whether we leave the apartment or not."

He sealed his lips over hers, and she was no longer shocked

by how quickly her body responded to the feel of his tongue sliding over hers. She felt her nipples harden and her skin flush hot. When their lips parted, she wanted to tug him in for another kiss, but she forced herself to behave.

"I brought you something." He took her hand and led her to the table, then reached into the box and pulled out a cat toy. "I brought this for Fifi. It's a crinkle ball, so it makes noise. I thought it might be easy for her to track, and I got her a mouse that has bells on it, too." He reached into the box and pulled out another cat toy.

Ally's heart melted as he handed her the toys. "You thought of Fifi."

He wrinkled his brow. "She's your pet. Of course I think of her."

Ally sank down to the couch. It wouldn't matter what else they did tonight. This was already up there as one of the best dates ever. "This is so thoughtful, and you knew just what to get her. Thank you."

Fifi brushed against his leg, and he reached for her, nuzzling the kitty against his chin. He kissed the white spot on her head, then looked into her unseeing eyes.

"How about it, Fifi? Are you ready to have a little fun?" He sat beside Ally and set Fifi on the floor so he could help Ally open Fifi's gifts.

"She's going to love these. You should see what she can do with the plastic top to a two-liter bottle of soda. It keeps her entertained for hours." Ally smiled up at him. "I love that you knew to get her noisy toys."

"I have to admit, I stood in the pet store for a while trying to figure out what was best, and I thought about my mom. When she first lost her sight, she said the most difficult thing was realizing that when she turned her head, she wouldn't see the source of the noises she heard. After being sighted for so long, I could only imagine what that must have been like. It didn't take her long to hone her other senses, but the thing that struck me those first few weeks was how much sound meant to her."

"For Fifi, too," Ally said. It was a strange coincidence that Heath's mother *and* her cat were blind. *Coincidence or fate?* Now she was just getting ahead of herself.

"That's what I thought. My mother losing her sight gave me a whole new understanding of what it's like to be blind. I never realized that when people who are blind take public transportation or even walk down the street, the sounds of other people provide guidance and helpful clues as to their surroundings. One of my mother's friends who is blind said that when she takes a train, she follows the sounds of the other passengers to gauge the edge of the track, how close the train is, when to board. Of course she uses other indicators, and her cane, but it really opened my eyes. That's what led me to think of the crinkle ball and the mouse with the bells. Fifi can track the sounds as she pushes them across the floor."

Ally shook the mouse, and Fifi lifted her head, as if she could see the toy. Heath lowered himself to the hardwood and batted the ball with Fifi for a few minutes before she took off across the floor with her new toy.

"I brought you something, too." Heath stood and reached into the box, withdrawing two medical journals. "There's a few months' worth in here. They're mostly ortho related, but there are a few other topics. I thought you might want to look through them."

"Really? Don't you need these?" She dug through the box

with her heart beating so fast she felt like it was Christmas morning.

"I've read them, and I'm happy to share."

She wrapped her arms around him, went up on tiptoes, and kissed him again. "This is so nice of you. Thank you! I never would have figured this surprise out in a million years, and it's just about the best surprise ever. I'm tempted to sit here and read instead of going out."

Heath hugged her close. "We can do that if you'd rather. There's a movie in there, too. It's one of my favorites. *Patch Adams*, with Robin Williams."

"Really?" She found the movie under a few of the journals. "I haven't seen this in years. I *love* this movie." She glanced over the couch at Fifi pawing at her new toy. "Would you be terribly disappointed if we just hung out here and watched this?"

"Sweetheart." He sank down to the couch and pulled her onto his lap. "Nothing you do could ever disappoint me. I just want to spend time with you and to see you happy."

Ally felt her heart opening a little more. She touched his five-o'clock shadow, which was too sexy not to press her lips to. Twice.

"Where did you come from, Heath Wild?"

He narrowed his eyes and said, "The better question is, what took us so long to find each other?"

Chapter Eleven

HEATH SLID A tray of biscuits into the oven while Ally stirred a pot of spaghetti sauce. He slid his hand around her waist and kissed her cheek, then moved to the cutting board and began chopping mushrooms. After they'd decided to stay in to watch the movie, they'd walked to the market down the street and picked up a few fresh vegetables and other ingredients to make homemade spaghetti sauce for their pasta dinner. Since they were short on time, they went with what Heath called his old fallback sauce, which involved crushed tomatoes, mushrooms, olive oil, garlic, basil, and other seasonings.

"Do you cook often?" Ally asked as he tossed a handful of chopped mushrooms into a pan with some olive oil.

He shrugged, stirring the mushrooms. "Not often and not well. We cook for my mom when we visit, but I'm usually running late, so sometimes I pick up takeout to keep everyone from having to wait too long to eat. After work I usually grab something quick for dinner, but I cook a few times a week. What about you?"

"I'm not a great cook, but I'm not picky, so I usually whip something up after work. Not that what I make is edible by other people's standards. You should remember that if you ever expect me to cook for you." She watched for his reaction. She really wasn't a great cook, and she figured it was better that he found that out now.

"Then between you and me, we'll be eating a lot of sub-standard, quick meals." He folded her into his arms. "Good thing food isn't the most important part of a relationship."

"What is the most important part?" She wrapped her arms around his waist and slid them up the back of his untucked dress shirt.

His lips curved in a devilish grin. "You mean there are more important things than good sex?"

She swatted his chest.

"I'm kidding. Communication, compromise, having things in common in *and* out of the bedroom." He turned his attention to the sauce, and his tone became serious. "Then there are the key elements, the things that build the foundation of trust. Like honesty and compassion. The ability to put someone else's needs ahead of your own."

She leaned against the counter and listened to him reel off all of the things she'd been thinking about lately. "For a guy who's so up on what it takes to build a good relationship, you've gone a long time without one."

He lifted his brows, still looking at the sauce.

"I have, too," she added. "I think the things you mentioned are all keys to a successful relationship, but it's interesting that we both reacted to being hurt in the same way." She took plates from the cabinet and worked with Heath to drain the pasta and serve dinner.

Heath poured them each a glass of wine, and when they finally settled onto the barstools at the counter to eat, he took her hand and kissed the back of it.

"I think there are two ways to react to being burned. People either protect themselves, which usually means putting up some sort of barriers against being hurt again—some thick and rigid, some more flexible—or they chalk it up as part of life and try to be more careful next time. I'm a wall builder. Obviously, you're a wall builder, too."

She picked up her wineglass. "Here's to tearing down those walls."

Hers seemed to be *crashing* down lately.

After they ate, Heath got up to do the dishes.

"I'll get those," she said, coming around the counter to help.

"I've got it. You can look through the journals, or play with Fifi. I actually like doing dishes. It's relaxing for me." Fifi rubbed up against his leg, and he smiled as he glanced down at her.

"Relaxing? Want to come over every evening about this time? I can arrange for a little relaxation time."

He dried his hands on a towel and set the plate he was washing aside, then picked up Fifi and stroked her fur. "Yes, actually. That's exactly what I want to do."

Their eyes locked, and for a moment Ally forgot how to breathe. His voice was dead serious, and the look in his eyes was equally earnest. Seeing him with Fifi did funny things to her, and Ally realized that she was falling for her *not-so-one-night* stand.

He kissed Fifi and set her down at his feet again. "Don't freak out on me. I'm not turning into a possessive guy who is always around."

She hooked her finger in the waist of his pants. "But you want to be around more."

He closed his eyes for a second and sighed. When he met her gaze again, he smiled and shrugged. "Is that so bad?"

"No. I like spending time with you. But I'm not an exciting

person. You might get bored of me."

He gathered her in his arms again—she loved the way he kept her close. "No chance, sweetheart. You're not a plaything. You're someone I admire." He kissed her softly. "You're someone I enjoy talking to and spending time with." He kissed her again, then patted her butt. "Go do something else or we'll end up in your bed again, and I need to prove to you that our relationship is deeper than oral and orgasms."

She laughed. "But you have to admit, the sex *is* amazing."

"More than amazing," he agreed.

Ally put the movie in the DVD player, chuckling about *oral and orgasms*, then sat down with a medical journal and thumbed through it while Heath finished washing the dishes. Then they snuggled on the couch to watch the movie. They laughed a lot, though Ally cried when one of the characters was killed. Heath was quiet, sitting with his feet up on the coffee table, with Ally tucked beneath his arm. She felt so comfortable with him she wasn't embarrassed by her tears. It was as if they'd been cooking dinners and watching movies together forever. Fifi crashed in her bed beside the couch, and as Ally wiped her tears, she noticed Heath's eyes were suspiciously damp, too. When the movie ended, Heath was uncharacteristically quiet.

"You okay?" she asked.

"Yes. I was just thinking of my father. I forgot about the part of the movie where his friend was killed." He shifted uncomfortably. "I'm not sure if I mentioned it, but my father was killed a few years ago during a home invasion, while trying to protect my mother."

Ally's heart squeezed. "I didn't know. I'm so sorry." She pulled her legs up beneath her on the couch and moved closer to him. "Did they catch the person who did it?"

"The police didn't, but my younger brother Logan did. He's a private investigator. He'd been tracking the guy when the guy broke into another house, where a woman and her young child were sleeping." He paused and seemed to be weighing what he was going to say next. When he spoke, his tone was grave, his eyes sad. "The police didn't act fast enough, but Logan did. He saved them."

This was what nightmares were made of. She imagined his brother following some crazy man into a house, knowing he had killed his father and blinded his mother, and the rage he must have felt. She could tell that Heath was holding something back, and she couldn't stop herself from asking, "And the guy?"

"Logan took care of him. Logan's not a cold-blooded killer, but the guy had a knife to the woman's throat. He didn't have a choice but to kill him or the guy might have killed that woman and her child." He drew in a deep breath, and his brows knitted together. "I haven't shared that with anyone. I didn't mean to lay it on you like that." He scrubbed his hand down his solemn face and pulled her into his arms.

"Heath, that's awful. And poor Logan, but at least he saved that woman and her child, and now your family knows that guy isn't lurking around somewhere."

He pressed her closer to him and nodded against her cheek. "My job is to help people, but if I had been Logan, I would have probably done the same thing."

She gazed into his eyes and saw a well of sadness. "Your father would be proud of him, and I'm sure he would have been proud of each of you, too, for taking such good care of your mother."

"Some people go their whole lives trying to gain their parents' approval. We had it since the day we were born."

The longing in his voice nearly did her in.

"You all must miss him terribly."

"We do. Enough time has passed that losing my father has become part of who I am, rather than all-consuming. The first few weeks after he was killed were rough. I was so angry and so worried about my mother. Not only about her safety, but for her emotional state as well. She's a strong woman, and she tried to put up a good front, refusing to move from our childhood home after our father was killed and assuring us she was okay. How can anyone be okay after losing the person they love most?"

Ally swallowed against the thickening in her throat.

"As time passed, things got easier. My mother really is a remarkable woman. I don't know how she's gone through losing the only man she ever loved to a random act of violence and losing her vision, and still she gives more than she'll ever ask for." His lips curved in a tentative smile. "She still sees the good all around her, even without sight." His brows knitted together. "I don't mean to be so maudlin."

"Heath, please. I've learned more about you in the last ten minutes than in the last two days. Well, not really, but almost." She pressed her lips to his. "I like that you're sharing this part of yourself with me. Your dad sounds like he was a wonderful man, and I'm sorry I didn't get a chance to meet him."

"He would have liked you a lot." Heath moved to the edge of the couch. "I should get going and let you get some rest."

Ally felt closer to Heath than ever, and she wanted him to stay with her, even if just to sleep, though she'd like to do more. But she knew she was falling for him much harder than she thought possible after only a few days, and she didn't trust herself not to tip over the edge and drown in a pool of emotions she wasn't sure she was ready for.

They kissed good night, and after he closed the door, she leaned her back against it, wishing he hadn't left. She peered out the peephole and saw him standing, arms crossed, eyes serious. He took a step back toward the door, then ran his hand through his hair and turned to leave.

She looked at the couch where he'd opened up to her, the kitchen where they'd cooked dinner, to the bed just beyond, where they'd made love. She should be filled to the hilt with those warm memories, but as she bent to pick up Fifi and smelled Heath's cologne on her fur, she missed Heath too much to feel anything other than lonely.

Chapter Twelve

THURSDAY EVENING HEATH pushed open the doors of NightCaps and took a quick visual sweep of the crowd, searching for his brothers. His eyes landed on his buddy Dylan Bad, the owner of NightCaps, standing behind the bar. Dylan waved, and Heath made his way toward him.

Dylan's dark eyes widened with his friendly smile. "Haven't seen you around much, Heath. How's it going?"

"Great, thanks. How're things with you? How're your brothers?" Like Heath, Dylan had three brothers. The Bads and the Wilds had grown up together, and they'd lived up to their names, spending their youths getting into mischief, although Heath had always been a little more careful than the rest of them. As the eldest, Heath had felt a responsibility toward keeping his younger siblings safe, and he'd taken that responsibility very seriously.

He nodded toward a table in the corner, where Mick Bad, Dylan's eldest brother, sat with Logan, Jackson, and Cooper.

"The Bads and the Wilds, at it again." Dylan laughed. He slid a bottle of beer across the bar to Heath. "Logan said you've got a girlfriend now."

Leave it to Logan to apply a little indirect pressure. Ever since he'd fallen in love with Stormy, who used to work at Dylan's bar, he'd been singing the praises of love and monogamy.

"Logan's right, although I'm not sure why he's talking about my personal life." Heath sipped his beer to hide the grin spreading across his lips from thinking about Ally.

"Cut him a break. He just said that you might blow them off to spend time with her." Dylan took the towel that had been hanging over his shoulder and wiped down the bar. He leaned closer and lowered his voice. "I wouldn't blame you. Spend time with a babe, or spend time with that crew? Easy choice in my eyes."

Heath laughed. "Thanks for the brew. Good to catch up." He crossed the crowded floor, weaving around tables and clusters of people and heading toward the sound of his brothers' laughter.

Logan turned just as Heath noticed Amanda, Ally's sister, sitting at a nearby booth with a guy who was wearing a suit and sitting pin straight, like he was on a job interview. Heath stopped midstride and looked around for Ally.

"Hey, bro. What's up? You look like you've seen a ghost." Logan pushed a chair out from the table with his foot. "Have a seat."

Heath shook off his surprise and sucked back his beer as he lowered himself onto the chair. Questions ricocheted through his mind, the most prominent being, *Where is Ally?* She'd said she was going out with her sister. Heath pulled out his cell to check the last few texts from her.

"Jackson and Coop were just telling us about that upcoming photo shoot for Sage Remington, that sculptor you like. Stormy wants to go, so I'm sure we'll rearrange our schedules to go. Why don't you and your *girlfriend* join us?"

Sage Remington was Heath's favorite sculptor. Normally

he'd be all over this opportunity, but he was too sidetracked over Ally to respond.

"I guess the zoo worked out for you, then?" Jackson asked.

"Zoo? What have I missed this week?" Cooper, their youngest brother, leaned across the table and eyed Heath. The top few buttons of his dress shirt were open. Cooper's tie hung loosely around his neck, and the new beard he'd been sporting lately gave him a swarthy look.

Heath let his brothers bounce their questions around for a while and quickly scanned his texts from Ally. None of them mentioned her plans for tonight. Of course they didn't. That would have been difficult to fit in between *I can't wait to get my hands on you again* and *Wear your favorite tie next time I see you*. He hadn't even thought to ask her about her plans again. He was tempted to call her, but he didn't want to look like a jealous asshole. Nor did he want to feel like one. But much to his dismay, he had the jealous part down pat.

"Cut him some slack. You guys are worse than my brothers." Mick lifted his beer and winked at Heath.

"Heath going out on a real date is newsworthy. I want to hear the zoo story." Cooper narrowed his midnight-blue eyes and leaned back in his chair. "Spill your guts, bro, or I for one will hassle you *all night long*." He said *all night long* really slowly, a sly smile spreading across his face.

Heath wanted to call Ally, or at least text her, without the pressure of his brothers hanging over his shoulder. He knew there had to be a reasonable explanation for her not being out with her sister tonight, but that didn't stop his gut from churning. He shoved his phone in his pocket rather than try to iron things out right this second. He eyed Amanda and then turned his attention back to his brothers.

"You want the scoop?" he asked Cooper.

"Heck, yeah," Cooper said. "Jackson and I shot a lingerie commercial at the zoo once. Remember that, Jackson? That was some freaky shit. We hooked up with the models afterward."

"*That* was some freaky shit," Jackson said with a smirk.

"Well, there wasn't any freaky shit to speak of on our date. We walked around the zoo at night. End of story." He sucked back his beer, unable to resist texting Ally. He was about to pull out his phone when Logan drew his brows together and leaned closer.

"Something wrong?" Logan asked.

Heath shook his head. "Nope."

"I told you," Logan said. "Give me a little background info and I can have everything you want to know in ten minutes."

"I'm good. Thanks." He trusted Ally, didn't he?

Yes, I trust her. I trust her completely.

That didn't stop his gut from twisting into a knot. He'd believed that the reason he didn't want a relationship was because women were too clingy and because he didn't want to get hurt. But what he'd forgotten was what it felt like to *worry* about being hurt. How could he turn off this awful feeling?

He pulled out his phone and sent Ally a text. *Miss you and wish you were here.*

"Texting zoo girl?" Cooper asked. "What's her name, anyway?"

"Allyson Jenner. She goes by Ally." Just saying her name made him feel better.

"Ally, nice name. So where is she tonight?" Jackson asked. "You could have brought her along."

"Allyson Jenner? Amanda Jenner's sister? Sexy as hell, dark hair?" Mick asked.

Heath felt his shoulders rise with tension. "That would be her."

"Her sister, Amanda, is our paralegal. She's on a date with some guy from our building. That's why I'm here. When she told me she was going out on her first date with him, I thought I'd keep an eye on her. She's a sweet girl, and you know how we lawyers are." He winked again, then nodded in Amanda's direction.

"Aw, how cute," Cooper said. "Mick is playing chaperone for his paralegal."

Heath's phone vibrated. Logan didn't miss a thing. His head snapped around as Heath read the text from Ally. *Me too. Miss you. My sister blew me off.*

"Ha-ha." Mick shook his head. "With guys like you roaming the streets, women have to be careful."

Jackson laughed. "Coop's harmless."

"Does that smile mean things are okay?" Logan asked Heath.

"No. It means I'm an asshole." He texted Ally. *She's at NightCaps with some guy. I'm here with my brothers. Want to meet us?*

"Why are you an asshole?" Logan asked.

Heath was thirty-four years old and telling his younger brother that he'd been nervous about something that he had no business being nervous about was like eating crow. No thank you.

"Where's Stormy tonight?" Heath asked in an effort to change the subject.

"She and a girlfriend went out to dinner," Logan answered.

"I can't imagine how good it must feel for her not to have to hide anymore, after hiding from that crazy ex-boyfriend for so long," Heath said.

"It's like night and day, but I forgot what it was like to care about someone enough to get jealous." Logan took a long swig of his beer.

"That's why it's better to play the field," Jackson said. "No ties, no worries."

"Wait, *you're* jealous?" Heath could hardly believe that Logan, the guy who'd had a hard time feeling anything but guilt after coming back from war, had fallen in love, much less was jealous.

"Hell yes. You've seen Stormy." Logan smirked. "She's fucking hot as hell."

"I want to photograph her, but *jealous boy* won't let me," Cooper said. "Jackson and I could get her a gig modeling. I'm sure of it. But Logan's too possessive."

"True," Jackson agreed.

"But you trust her," Heath said.

"Hell yes, I trust her. What does that have to do with anything?" Logan looked at the vibrating cell phone in Heath's hand. "Is that why you look like you've got a crowbar up your ass? You're jealous over Ally?"

"Shit." Heath shook his head, though he knew by the laughter around the table that his brothers and Mick saw right through him. "Okay, fine. Yes, okay? What the hell do you want from me?"

Logan patted him on the back. "I told you, bro. Forget everything you thought you knew about yourself, because when love comes knockin', you got no choice but to be home."

"Two brothers fallen, Jackson. Here's to remaining single." Cooper held his beer bottle up, and Jackson tapped it with his. "Mick?"

Mick's eyes were locked on Amanda and her date. "Huh? Sorry."

"I think Ally's sister has an admirer," Logan said to Heath.

Heath arched a brow at Mick, who shook his head and said, "She works for me."

"So?" all four Wild brothers said at once.

"On that note, I think I'll go grab another beer from Dylan." Mick looked around the table. "Anyone else want one?"

Cooper nudged Jackson. "Check out the two blondes at the bar." He and Jackson joined Mick, leaving Logan and Heath alone.

Heath read Ally's text.

I don't want to spoil your fun. I'm reading one of the journals you gave me.

It was just like her to put him first.

"Tell her to meet us," Logan said.

"You read my text message?"

"No. I read the look on your face. Heath, being jealous is totally normal. Missing her is normal. If you're like me, you're sitting here trying to have a good time when you really want to be with her. Don't you think I would rather be with Stormy every minute of the day?"

Heath shrugged. "I assume you would, but what do I know?"

"You know more than you think you do."

"Logan." Heath scrubbed his hand down his face in frustration. "Ally has become everything to me way too fast. I think about her when I wake up. I want to be with her the minute I leave work, and the messed-up part is that I trust her explicitly, when the way we met should totally nix that idea from the get-go."

"One-night stand?"

One quick nod gave Logan his answer.

"Big shit. Stormy and I started off with hate sex."

"Hate sex? What does that mean?" Heath asked.

"Sex to escape all the stuff in life that you hate. You know, get it out of your system." Logan wrinkled his brow. "Okay, so you probably *don't* know hate sex. That's not really your thing, but that's how we started. So what? Would it have been better if we'd started on a blind date? Would I love her more? Trust her more? Care for her more? Hell no. Life isn't neat. Why should relationships be?"

"That's just it," Heath admitted. "I don't think I could care for her more than I do, and then the next day comes, and that feeling just gets bigger. Now I'm sitting here itching to see her, and I've become the clingy bitch I avoided all these years."

Logan's blue eyes twinkled with a brotherly taunt. "Shit, look at you. Man, don't tell Coop and Jackson that. They'll eat you alive. But I get it." He lowered his voice. "Don't you think I'm wondering how many guys are checking out Stormy right now? Even though I know she's coming home to me, my gut's on fire."

"Join the club." Heath inhaled a deep breath and blew it out fast. "Listen, tell Thing One and Thing Two I'll see them at Mom's Sunday, and tell Mick goodbye. I'm going to take off. You're a bigger man than me, bro. I can't sit here wanting to be with her for another second when my legs work just fine." He patted his brother's shoulder as he stood to leave. "Thanks, Logan. I needed to hear every word you just said."

"Who would have thought you'd learn a lesson from your younger brother?"

"Logan, you've taught me more about bravery and loyalty in the last few years than anyone else ever could." He tipped his chin as a way of saying goodbye *and* thank you, and headed for his woman.

Chapter Thirteen

ALLY PEERED THROUGH the peephole of her apartment door and her heart skipped a beat at the sight of Heath pacing the hallway. Before pulling the door open, she allowed herself an extra second to gawk. His jaw was tight, and his eyes were trained on the ground, as if he were mulling something over or was annoyed. He rubbed the back of his neck and grimaced. She wondered if something had happened with his brothers. It had been a while since she'd texted him about not meeting him at NightCaps.

She opened the door, and the second he lifted his eyes, all that tension seemed to melt from his body and float away. His full, beautiful lips curved up, and his gaze softened as he reached for her. There was a tingling in the pit of her stomach as one arm circled her waist while the other wrapped around her back and pulled her against him.

"You're supposed to be out with your brothers."

"I missed you too much to stay away a second longer." The emotion emanating off of him was different from the fierce sexuality she was used to. The way he was looking at her spoke of the bond she felt forming between them.

Ally couldn't deny the thundering of her heart at the realization that he had to be falling for her just as hard as she was falling for him. Fear tiptoed through her at the thought. As his lips met hers, her body filled with a light, dreamy emotion that made her feel warm and wonderful all over and swept that fear away. Everything Heath did and said made her feel and think in ways that were new and immensely meaningful and *real*.

She closed her eyes and reveled in the warmth of his lips brushing over her cheek and his breath whispering over her skin.

"I just had to be with you. We don't have to make love. I just need the closeness."

Ally didn't even try to speak. She knew her voice wouldn't come. Instead, she took his hand and led him into the apartment. She hadn't ever spent the night with a man in this apartment, and the thought of doing so with Heath thrilled and terrified her.

He ran his hands over the curve of her hips, his gaze never leaving hers, and the air around them pulsed with too many emotions to decipher.

"I want to stay," he whispered.

"I'm afraid." As soon as the words left her lips she regretted them.

"Of?" He didn't loosen his grip or step back. His eyes filled with empathy, and that drew her further in.

"Falling for you."

His hands came up and warmed her cheeks. "Honesty will get you everywhere." He kissed her forehead. "Do you not want to fall for me?"

"It's not that. I can't help myself from falling for you, but this is so fast. We've talked about this." She nibbled on her lower lip, wondering why she was pushing away the only man she'd ever felt this much for. He was a good man, an honest man, a man she *wanted* to wake up next to.

A sweet, easy smile stretched across his face as he dropped his hands back down to her waist. "How about if I don't let you fall for me?"

She pressed her forehead to his chest. "Everything you do makes me fall harder. Just the way you're looking at me makes my heart go crazy." She gazed up at him and he was still smiling, which made her heart squeeze even more. "We shouldn't spend the night together."

There. She'd said it.

She felt horrible and immediately wished she hadn't said it. But for some stupid reason, she needed to be one hundred percent sure that she was ready to take this step before finding herself in Heath's arms in the morning.

"Because you're afraid of falling for me?" His eyes grew serious.

She nodded, knowing that if she agreed aloud, it would feel wrong, too.

He drew her in closer and pressed his hand to the back of her head. She felt his heart beating against her cheek. He felt so good, so safe. So loving. She was too emotional to separate how right he felt from the fear that had tiptoed back in.

"Okay." He drew back and inhaled a long, even breath, then pulled his shoulders back. His brows knitted together as he readied himself for something.

Her insides twisted into a tight knot. "Okay?"

"I'm not going to push you into something you're not ready for. I want to be with you. I'm ready, and I don't care how fast it is, but that doesn't mean you have to be on the same page with me. If you're not ready, you're not ready." He caressed her cheek and pressed his lips to hers. "I'll take what time I can get until you realize that this is the real thing."

"I don't know that I'm *not* ready to wake up in your arms. I just don't know if I *am* ready." She turned away and shook her head. "I sound ridiculous."

He pulled her into his arms again, and his smile warmed her. "You're not ridiculous. You're careful. I appreciate that, because I don't know how to slow down this bullet train, and I'm not sure I want to. So it's probably good that you're careful."

"So, what now?"

He took a step back. "Now I cool my jets and let you have some space to think things over."

She gripped his forearms. "You're leaving?"

"Sweetheart, if I stay, I'm not going to want to leave. And if I make love to you, then I *really* won't want to leave. Maybe a one-night break is a good thing. We can both clear our heads. Can I see you tomorrow night?"

"Of course." She was too conflicted to think straight. "But I don't want you to leave."

He tucked her hair behind her ear. "But you don't want me to stay, either, and as much as I have to protect your heart, I also need to protect mine."

Chapter Fourteen

FRIDAY BROUGHT SUNSHINE *and* conflict. Two opposing forces that wreaked havoc with Ally's mind. On her way to meet Amanda for lunch, Ally read through the thread of texts she and Heath had exchanged over the morning.

Heath: *Good morning, beautiful. Missed you last night.*

Ally: *I missed you, too. Can't wait to see you tonight.*

An hour later…

Heath: *What do you want to do tonight?*

Ally: *You.*

Heath: *Shouldn't you wine and dine me first?*

Ally: *If you're into that sort of thing, sure.*

Heath: *I'm more than a sex machine. I think I'll wine and dine you. Do you like clubs or someplace quiet?*

Ally: *Your choice. I just want to be with you.*

Heath: *Careful, sweetheart. That sounds an awful lot like you're falling for me.*

Ten minutes ago…

Heath: *How about if we go to my place after dinner?*

You've never been there.

Ally's pulse quickened at the idea of entering Heath's private lair. Part of her saw spending time at her apartment as having a modicum of control, only she hadn't realized that until she'd read his text, and now, relinquishing control to Heath was surprisingly easier than it had been last night.

Ally: *Yes. But I still don't think I can stay over.*
Heath: *Way to kill a guy's hopes.*

Ally walked into the café around the corner from the hospital to meet Amanda and sent a quick response.

Keep hoping. You never know when I'll change my mind.

She stood just inside the doorway of the café, surveying the tables and booths, looking for Amanda. The line to the counter at the opposite end of the café ran along the wall to her left and stopped just a few feet short of where she stood.

"Ally!"

She spotted Amanda in a booth by the wall. The heels of Ally's boots *clicked* as she made her way to the booth and slid in across from Amanda.

"I didn't see you. Sorry." She set her purse behind her and eyed Amanda, whose blouse was unbuttoned lower than usual. When they'd spoken in the morning, Amanda had said that her date was a dud. He'd been cute and sweet, but *too* nice. Ally didn't know a guy could be too nice for Amanda. For her? Sure. But for her conservative sister? She needed details.

"*What* is up with you?"

Amanda's eyes widened. "Nothing is *up*." She straightened

her napkin on her lap, and when her name was called, indicating their food was ready, she jumped up to get their order. "I've got it."

Ally hadn't seen Amanda look so excited in a long time. She watched her sister hustle across the floor in a pair of black heels that were higher than what she usually wore. She knew her sister reserved these particular sexy heels for special occasions. With them, Amanda wore a tight black skirt that accentuated her tiny waist, and if Ally wasn't mistaken—which, after twenty-six years, she surely was not—her sister's ass swayed in a way that had *available* written all over it.

What the hell?

"Here we go." Amanda set the tray on the table and slid into the booth, handing Ally the salad she'd ordered for her. She smiled and tucked her hair behind her ear, while Ally tried not to sneer at the two guys checking out her sister from a nearby table.

"Here we go? Like I didn't just watch some sex kitten who used to be my conservative sister slink up to the counter?" Ally smiled as she stabbed a tomato and pointed it at Amanda. "What happened to you last night?"

Amanda shrugged. "I don't know. Jeb was really sweet. He was smart and funny and nice."

"Yeah, you gave me that already. Too nice, if I remember correctly."

"Right. *Too* nice. And it got me thinking." Amanda took a bite of her salad.

"Are you going to clue me in, or am I supposed to guess this part?"

"Remember Kevin?"

"Boring Kevin? How could I forget?" Amanda had dated

Kevin for two months. He was so quiet that Ally had thought he was mute the first time she'd met him.

"And do you remember M.J.?"

Ally rolled her eyes. Another boring boyfriend Amanda had dated for a few weeks.

"Right. Well, what do my previous boyfriends tell you about me?"

"That you like boring guys?"

"No, that I'm a boring-guy magnet. Whereas you're a hot-guy magnet." She raised her brows. "Speaking of hot guys. I saw your man walk out of NightCaps last night."

"Yeah, I know. We can go back to him in a sec." She set a serious stare on Amanda. "Tell me about *you*. You do realize that you've sexed yourself up enough that guys will expect more from you than hand-holding and fluttering eyelashes, right?"

"I am the older sister, you know." Amanda set down her fork and wiped her mouth, then folded her hands in her lap and pulled her shoulders back. "I'm just testing the waters. Last night one of the partners in my firm, Mick Bad, was at NightCaps. I told him I was going there on a date with a guy from our building, and then I saw him up at the bar with some other guys, and he kept stealing glances at me. Mick's a real sex machine. I mean, our female clients dress in six-inch heels when they have meetings with him, and I know it's for his benefit."

"Mandy, those women can probably handle six-inch heels and sex-machine guys. But you're not *that* girl."

"Relax. I don't want to sleep with Mick." She waved her hand dismissively. "Or maybe I do, but I *won't*. He's way out of my league. But it made me think about what I do want. I liked that he was looking at me last night. I like the *way* he was looking at me. I was more intrigued by him than my date.

So…" She motioned toward her outfit. "I'm running an experiment. To see what happens if I dress a little sexier."

Ally shifted her gaze to the guys who were still eyeing Amanda, only now they were eyeing Ally, too.

"I'd say you're definitely gaining a wider audience. Are you sure you want to do this? I'm not sure you can handle the kind of guys you're going to attract. You have a killer body, you know."

Amanda blushed. "Thank you, but just because I gain attention doesn't mean I have to go out with the guys. I'll be careful. I promise."

"Well, I can't say it's a bad look for you. You're totally hot, but I know what dressing provocatively can bring on, and I don't want you to get hurt."

"I get it. Okay. Now can we move on?" She touched Ally's hand. "What's up with your guy?"

"My guy." Ally sighed. "I really, really like my guy."

"You're gushing. You never gush."

"I know. I'm conflicted and I'm not conflicted at the same time, which makes no sense." She met her sister's curious gaze.

"I'm really good at deciphering things, you know. Maybe I can help. What's got you worried?" Amanda crossed her arms and settled back in the booth.

"How much I feel and how fast I feel it." Ally glanced at the people walking by, trying to determine why it was bothering her that she and Heath were moving fast.

"That would probably throw me for a loop, too, but you know fast is how you are in everything you do. You knew with your last boyfriend that he was going to be a long-term boyfriend right away, but you also knew he wasn't *the one*."

"My cheating ex?" She'd stopped using his name after they

broke up.

"Yes, but you knew he wasn't the guy you were going to marry. You told me that the first week you dated him. You said he wasn't marriage material but he was more than a few nights' material, remember?"

"No." Ally didn't remember saying that, but she did remember feeling that way.

"I think you're pretty intuitive. You knew you wanted the job at the hospital after talking to the HR person over the phone. And you have always said that you get a feeling about things and you follow your gut, so what does your gut tell you?"

"That's the problem." Ally pushed her salad around on her plate with her fork, no longer hungry. "*Every* part of me wants *more*. More time with him, more time to get to know him. But it scares the heck out of me. What if I'm wrong? What if we spend more time and then…I don't know, it just goes to shit?"

Amanda shrugged one shoulder. "I'm the careful one, remember?"

"Mandy, I need your help."

"No, you don't. Not really. You need to figure out your pros and cons. What do you have to gain?"

"Possibly the happiest, greatest feeling of my life on a daily basis." Ally couldn't suppress her smile at the thought of spending more time with Heath, but as Amanda asked what she had to lose, her smile faded.

"Lose? You mean my cons list? What if I get hurt?" The knot in her stomach tightened.

"What if you do? Don't all relationships have that risk? And why are you being so careful anyway? You usually make a decision and go with it."

"I'm afraid of getting hurt."

"You've been hurt before and you survived. How is this different?"

Ally chewed on that question for a few minutes, trying to figure out why she was hesitating. When the realization hit, it stung like a swarm of bees.

"Because this time I care. I'm falling in love with him, and I've never been in love before."

"Oh, Ally." Amanda reached across the table and took her sister's hand. "If you're really falling for him, then that's a wonderful thing. You're *supposed* to feel scared and wonderful at the same time. Trust me. I've done my research. I've read every romance novel written in the last ten years, watched every romantic movie, and sat in the wings of life longingly watching couples that are in love."

"Aw, Mandy…" She squeezed her sister's hand, and when her sister waved her off, obviously not wanting her pity, Ally said, "So you don't think I'm crazy?"

Amanda laughed. "You're one of the sanest people I know. Okay, this is the truth." She narrowed her eyes and lowered her chin in the listen-to-me-baby-sister way she always had. "I might give you shit about your sexual escapades, which I know are not that plentiful but scare me all the same, because you're my sister and I never want anything bad to happen to you. But you're out there living life, following your desires. You know what you like and what you don't like, and I don't just mean sexually. You're that way with life in general, and that's a huge thing. So whatever you're feeling for Heath is probably *very* real. I might be older than you, but I'm only now beginning to even think about those things. And even just dressing differently today was empowering. I'm beginning to understand what you've known all along."

"Really?" Ally soaked in her sister's praise, so thankful for her honesty that she felt near tears.

"Really."

"I don't want to be blamed if you meet creeps. In fact, you should tell me where you go with your dates so I can keep an eye on you."

"Hopefully you'll be too busy with Mr. Right to hang around watching me."

Mr. Right.

She'd never really contemplated finding Mr. Right. Then again, she'd never contemplated adopting a blind kitty until she'd found Fifi, either—and she'd never once regretted adopting her.

Maybe some things are meant to be.

Chapter Fifteen

HEATH HADN'T BEEN able to take his eyes off of Ally all evening. Not while they ate dinner, not while they walked through the city, and not now, as he hailed a cab to take them to his mother's house. She looked too damn sexy in a form-fitting black dress that skimmed her knees. Everything about her was mesmerizing, from the way she twirled her hair when she was nervous to the way her eyes lit up when she spoke about her sister and parents. As he draped an arm over her shoulder and they watched a cab approach, he still couldn't pinpoint what it was about her that had completely enraptured him from the start. And he no longer cared. Being with Ally was right as rain, and he wasn't going to pick it apart or look for holes in it.

All day he'd been looking forward to seeing her and bringing her further into his life. He'd almost asked Logan to take his place visiting his mother tonight, but at the last minute he'd realized that if he really wanted Ally in his life, she had to accept all of him, including the time he dedicated to his family. Ally had actually sounded excited to meet her.

"Are you sure you're still okay with stopping by my mom's?"

"Of course. I can't wait to meet the woman who raised you." She smiled and touched his cheek. She touched him a lot, and it never failed to make him smile. He loved how affectionate she was and how nothing felt forced or unnatural.

"From everything you've told me, your mother sounds pretty incredible." She took a step back as the cab pulled up.

Heath held the door for Ally. "Four rambunctious boys, each two years apart? She had her hands full."

He tried to ignore the fact that Ally's dress inched up when she sat down. She gazed up at him through thick lashes, her hair tumbled over her shoulders in loose curls, and her seductive femininity was too potent to resist. He slid a hand to the nape of her neck and pulled her in closer. He brushed his lips over hers, gently covering her mouth, and when she responded, he devoured her softness. Taking every breath she was willing to give, he deepened the kiss, and his hand touched the edge of her dress. He fought the urge to touch her, to seek her heat, and he was surprised by his own restraint.

As their lips parted, her eyes remained closed, and he wanted her more than ever. But he wanted more than the cheap thrill of touching her or taking her over the edge in the back of a cab. He wanted that, too. Of course he did. Naughtiness was part of their relationship. They both knew it. But everything was changing in his heart and his mind, and the thought of the cabdriver seeing her midorgasm made his gut twist with jealousy.

In that moment Heath knew that everything had changed.

He'd completely fallen in love with Ally, and he never wanted to look back.

HEATH'S MOTHER'S HOUSE was not what Ally had imagined for a family of six. The small, two-story had a long driveway and sat among other similar houses, with a narrow front porch and two dormers on the second floor.

"This is where you grew up?" she asked.

"Yes. It seems small, right?" Heath asked as they followed a sidewalk from the driveway around to a postage-stamp-sized fenced-in backyard.

"A little."

"There's only one bedroom upstairs, which Logan and I shared. It was barely big enough for our bunk bed. Jackson and Cooper shared a bunk bed in the loft." He led her up a set of concrete steps to a small covered porch.

"Did you mind sharing a room?" She and Amanda had each had their own room growing up, and she wasn't sure she would have wanted the constant companionship of a roommate when she was a teenager.

"Sometimes, but it's probably why we're all so close. We had to work out our differences. There was no place to hide from them." He knocked on the door and peered in the window, before walking into a tidy modern kitchen.

"Mom?" he called toward the living room, which Ally could see through an arched opening as they passed through the kitchen.

"Heath? Honey? Is that you?" Heath's mother held on to the railing as she came down the stairs. She was a pretty woman, with dark shoulder-length hair and a warm smile. Her olive skin looked soft and youthful, though as Heath went to her side and Ally stepped closer, the fine lines around her eyes and the soft etching in her cheeks gave away her age.

"Yes, it is." With one hand on his mother's lower back, he held his other arm out to guide her as they descended the stairs to the living room.

"Ally is with you?" She lifted gray-blue eyes directly toward Ally.

Ally reached for her hand. "Hi. Yes, I'm right here."

"Hi, Ally. I'm Mary Lou. What a pleasure it is to meet you." She opened her arms and embraced her, holding her a moment longer than Ally expected.

"Won't you please have a seat?" She motioned toward the couch, still holding Heath's arm as he guided her around a recliner to an olive-green couch.

Ally sat in a recliner, and Health came to her side and placed a hand on her shoulder. Ally could feel nervous tension in his touch. She placed her hand over his to let him know she was okay.

"Heath tells me that you work at the hospital, too. In the lab," Mary Lou said. Before Ally could respond, she added, "Lovey, sit down. You're making me nervous."

"How do you know I'm not sitting in the other recliner?" Heath said as he sank down on the other side of the couch.

Mary Lou smiled and folded her hands in her lap. "Mothers have eyes everywhere."

Ally liked Mary Lou's easy nature. "My mother says that she knows where we are in her house at all times by the feel of the room."

"That is very true for me, too," Mary Lou said. "The minute my boys walk into the house, I can sense their moods. Take Heath, for example. He's been smiling since he arrived, yes?"

She glanced at the easy smile on Heath's face. "Yes, he has."

"But I can tell he's a little nervous, too," his mother added.

"Okay, thanks for that, Mom." Heath shook his head.

"Well, you are a little nervous, aren't you, honey?"

Heath sighed, and his mother waved dismissively in his

direction. "When Cooper, my youngest, comes over, he's a whirlwind of energy. I can always tell if he's had a bad day, because the whirlwind has a heaviness to it, and it has nothing to do with losing my sight. It was the same way when they were little. I could hear the door open after school, and from the sound of the feet on the hardwood I knew who it was. Heath's a careful stepper, soft and direct, while Logan's steps have always been determined." She turned toward Heath. "Don't you agree, lovey? And Jackson, he's a little complicated. He's either stealthy, like he's on the prowl, or he's determined."

"You have us nailed perfectly, but one day we'll surprise you," Heath said.

His mother reached over and felt her way along the cushion until her fingers met his leg, and she patted his thigh. "Sweetie, you boys surprise me every day." She turned her attention to Ally. "Getting back to our conversation, you work in the lab? Do you enjoy it?"

"Yes, very much so. Every day moves faster than the one before, and I really enjoy the patient contact." She thought about an elderly gentleman she'd taken blood from earlier that afternoon and how grumpy he'd been when she'd come into the room. He'd been in the hospital two weeks earlier, and Ally empathized with his displeasure at being stuck with another needle. He'd reminded her of her father, and when she'd noticed a book by her father's favorite author on the nightstand, she'd been able to put him at ease by discussing what her father liked about the author's writing style. He was smiling when she left, and she felt as though she'd brought a little sunshine to his bleak afternoon.

The roar of a motorcycle sounded out front.

"Sounds like Jackson is here," Mary Lou said. "I think he's

got something on his mind lately, but whatever it is, he's keeping it close to his chest."

"Jackson always has something on his mind." Heath rose as the front door flew open and a tall, handsome man strutted in wearing a leather jacket and a major case of helmet head. He shook his head like a puppy shakes off rain and then ran a hand through thick dark hair. He set the helmet he carried on a table by the door and lifted dark blue eyes to Heath, then shifted his gaze to Ally. A smile spread across his scruffy cheeks.

"Looks like I'm just in time for the party," Jackson said as he crossed the room. His jeans were tight across his hips, and the black biker boots he wore *clunked* on the hardwood floor. He held a hand out in greeting. "I'm Jackson. Heath's favorite brother."

Heath scoffed, but his smile told Ally that this was a familiar tease.

"Hi. I'm Ally." His hand was strong and firm, like Heath's.

"Nice to meet you." Jackson walked around the couch and leaned down to kiss Mary Lou's cheek. "Hi, Ma. Do you mind if I poke around the attic?"

"The attic? Whatever for?" she asked with a wrinkled brow.

"Remember that box of pictures I had from when Dad bought me my first camera?" Jackson asked. "The ones I developed in my darkroom?"

"You mean the ones you developed in the bathroom?" A sweet smile crossed her lips. "Sure, baby. Go ahead."

"Cool deal." He turned toward Heath. "Where are you guys heading tonight?"

"My place," Heath answered.

"Sounds fun. Remember, the invitation is open for you guys to join us at Remington's show in a few weeks. Ally might enjoy meeting a famous sculptor like Sage Remington up close and personal." Jackson smirked, and Ally knew he'd thrown that jab in about Sage Remington, one of the hottest, and best-looking, sculptors out there, just to annoy Heath.

She liked seeing the way Heath grimaced at the taunt.

"Thanks. Maybe we'll do that. Jackson is a photographer," Heath explained. "He's taking the promotional photos for Sage Remington's exhibit." He turned back to Jackson. "What are you going to do with the pictures?"

Jackson smiled. "I'm making a birthday present for Laney." He pointed to the stairs. "I'm heading up. Nice to meet you, Ally. Mom, you need anything from the attic?" Erica Lane had been Jackson's best friend since elementary school.

"No, honey. Thank you."

Jackson took the stairs two at a time, and Mary Lou let out a breath as she settled back again.

"So much for stealth," Mary Lou said. "Wow, he sounded more like Cooper than himself, didn't he? He must be up to something mischievous."

Ally smiled at the way she took her sons all in stride.

They talked for a while longer about Ally's family and were interrupted when Jackson came back downstairs with a big box of photos and set them on the coffee table.

"Who wants to see Heath's teenage years?" Jackson's eyes lit up, and Ally wanted to dive right in.

"*Christ.* Really, Jackson?" Heath scrubbed his hand down his face.

"Oh, honey." Mary Lou reached for him. "You have always been such a handsome devil."

Ally raised her brows and flashed Heath a flirtatious smile. He *was* handsome, *and* he was devilish in the bedroom. As she sank to the floor beside the coffee table and Jackson began handing her pictures of Heath and each of his brothers at various ages, Heath sat in the recliner behind her and spread his knees so she was sitting between them.

Mary Lou sat forward and lifted her chin. Ally knew she was listening for clues as to what they saw, and she ached with empathy for what Mary Lou would never have again: she was a mother no longer able to see the faces of the people she loved. Of course, working in a hospital gave her great perspective. Being blind had its hardships, but it wasn't cancer, which could steal a life without warning. At least Mary Lou was still here to spend time with her sons.

Being in Heath's childhood home and seeing photographs of his father on the wall and in the hutch by the dining room table would have been enough perspective on its own. Heath's mother had survived that horrible attack. Perspective was great, but it didn't lessen the sense of loss that Ally wondered if Mary Lou felt.

"I'm going to share these with your mom," she said quietly to Heath. She selected a handful of pictures and joined Mary Lou on the couch.

"Maybe you can help me figure out who each of the boys are in the pictures. I can recognize Heath by his expressive eyes, but I'm having trouble with the others."

"Thank you. I'll try. I've looked at these photos so many times through the years, I probably have most of them memorized."

Ally selected one of the pictures and handed it to Mary Lou. "This one has three teenagers. I know the one on the far left is Heath because he has a serious look in his eyes that I've seen quite often. I recognize your driveway, and Heath has on a pair of jeans and a striped shirt, which looks a little *Bert and Ernie* to me." She chuckled and looked up at Heath, who was gazing at her with so much love she wondered if Jackson and his mother could feel the emotion rolling off of him.

Jackson was stacking pictures beside the box. He followed Ally's gaze and shook his head. Obviously he could feel the love rolling off of Heath, and surprisingly, instead of being embarrassed, she loved it. Heath didn't react, but his lips curved in a sweet smile meant for Ally.

"He loved that shirt, and his brothers used to tease him relentlessly. It was his lucky shirt. One of his father's old shirts." Mary Lou leaned closer to Ally. "Does the shirt sort of hang off of him, like it's too big in the shoulders?"

"Yes, a little bit."

Mary Lou pressed her lips together and tilted her chin up, as if she were trying to remember something. "He was probably a junior in high school. He had a growth spurt that year and his father's shirts fit him a little better."

"That's about how old he looks. The other two boys are smiling. One has longer hair—it covers his ears—but the other is very clean-cut. Almost like he'd just come from the barber. They're both wearing jeans and sneakers."

"Their shirts, honey? What do they look like? The boys have always had very distinct taste."

"If it's a band shirt, it's probably me," Jackson said.

"Yes, one is a black shirt with an AC/DC logo. Is that you, Jackson?" Ally asked.

"Oh, that music. He used to listen to it so loud my ears would ring." Mary Lou reached up and touched her ears.

Jackson smiled, and it softened the look of concentration on his face. "You used to dance to it while you made dinner, Mom.

Don't try to pretend you didn't like it."

"It's true." Heath looked at Mary Lou, and his smile broadened. "Remember how long her hair was, Jackson?"

Jackson leaned an elbow on the coffee table. "Almost to her waist."

"Your father loved my long hair." Mary Lou reached up and touched her hair with a thoughtful look on her face.

"You still look beautiful, Mom," Heath said. "I also remember that you knew most of the words to the songs, too."

"Well, how could I not with how often Jackson played those albums?" She shook her head and smiled in Jackson's direction.

"I still do. Gotta love my vinyl." Jackson winked at Ally.

"That means the other one in the picture is probably Cooper," Mary Lou said. "Because Jackson and Cooper have always been like twins, doing everything together, while Logan would usually strike out on his own."

Heath moved to the empty cushion beside his mother and looked over her shoulder. "That's Coop, all right. And the reason his hair was so short is that he'd won that photo award contest in *Photography* magazine—remember, Ma? You made him get a haircut to accept his award."

Mary Lou smiled. "Yes, oh goodness. He was so upset with me over that haircut. But I couldn't let him accept an award looking like a ragamuffin."

Jackson rolled his eyes. "Every guy looked like that back then, Ma."

"Yes, well, I was proud of him. And he met that beautiful girl at the award ceremony, which I credit to the haircut." She lifted her shoulders quickly, as if to say, *See? It helped him after all.*

Heath shook his head. "Coop would have gotten that girl

with or without the haircut."

"Maybe so. But you never know." Mary Lou handed the photo back to Ally and asked, "Do you have more?"

The enthusiasm in her voice made Ally smile as she placed another picture in her hands.

They spent the next hour laughing and talking about Heath and his brothers' teenage years and their mischievous behavior. By the time Heath and Ally were ready to leave, Ally felt like Mary Lou and Jackson were old friends. They were both easygoing and warm. Jackson's personality was different from Heath's. As edgy as Jackson dressed, his personality was laid-back, while Heath had an intensity about him that made Ally's pulse quicken every time they were close.

Heath hugged his mother goodbye and promised to see her Sunday for dinner.

"Ally, will you be joining us on Sunday?" Mary Lou asked.

Ally looked up at Heath, not wanting to impose on his time with his family.

"I'd love it if you'd join us, but don't feel pressured if you have plans," Heath said.

Jackson lowered his voice, as if he were sharing a secret. "That means he wants you to come."

"Thank you, Mary Lou. I'd really enjoy that." She slid her hand around Heath's waist, feeling like she'd just stepped deeper into his inner circle—and loving it.

Chapter Sixteen

HEATH LIVED AT 200 Eleventh Avenue, one of the most luxurious condominiums in the city. He was a little embarrassed by the prestigious address as they entered the gunmetal-gray-colored building. Its impressive architecture included protruding piers and an arched and curved cornice with multi-paned windows. He'd purposefully not driven tonight. His was the only building with an en-suite garage, where cars were brought up on freight elevators to each residence. The extravagance was not something Heath had sought out, but he'd wanted the view of the Hudson River, and the twenty-four-foot ceilings and en-suite garage were part of the package.

"You must have a great view of the water," Ally said as they rode the elevator up to his apartment.

"I do, but the view in here is much more beautiful." He pulled her in close and kissed her neck. "Watching you with my family made me fall for you a little harder."

"I think you took me there hoping it would have the same effect on me."

"Not hoping, but I wondered if it might drive you away."

"Not on your life." She went up on her toes and kissed him.

The elevator doors opened, and with a hand on her lower back, he guided her into his living room. Her eyes went directly to the far wall, which boasted floor-to-ceiling bookshelves, complete with a sliding library ladder. The books were interspersed with family photographs and a few of Heath's favorite sculptures and vases.

Ally's eyes widened as she walked past the wall of windows overlooking the river, which she'd missed when she'd been so taken with the bookshelves, slowing for only a second to take in the glorious view before reaching the shelves. She ran her fingers over the spines of a row of books, then glanced over her shoulder at Heath.

"These shelves, all these books…It's like a dream come true." She took a few steps and stood before his favorite sculpture. Ally tilted her head to the right, then to the left, as she examined the sculpture of a woman's chest to forehead.

"I've never seen anything like this up close," Ally said with a hint of awe. "It's as if the steel is moving in the wind. I can almost feel this woman breathe and feel her hair blowing in the wind. It's fascinating."

"Sage Remington is the artist."

"I know of him, but I've never seen his work up close. We really should join Jackson when he does the shoot. What a treat that would be."

Treat? She had no idea that to Heath, she was the biggest treat of all.

"I'd like that. We'll plan to go." He admired the sculpture again. "He creates these using varying widths of steel ribbons. You see how there's no back? I think that gives the steel the feel of fluidity." He joined her by the sculpture. "It's the definition that gets me. The ability to define everything—her lips, her nose, the dips and swells of her neck. He somehow makes her look feminine and delicate despite the heavy metal he uses."

"Heath." She reached for his hand. "Why would you ever

want to stay at my place when you have all of this at your disposal? These books, this glorious art." She turned to face the river. "And this amazing view?" She shifted her gaze, and her eyes danced over the Scandinavian-style couches. Heath's apartment wasn't lavishly furnished, and much like Ally's, it wasn't littered with accessories. He lived simply, at a pricey address.

He ran his hands down her arms. "Isn't it obvious?"

"No," she said with wide eyes.

"Because you're there. This is stuff, Ally. Books, art, and a view. I'd rather wake up to you than wake up to the Hudson."

"If that's a line, you really have mastered the art of seduction."

His thumb brushed lightly over her lower lip. He'd waited all night to be closer to her, and now she was looking at him with her big, beautiful eyes, touching his stomach with her delicate hand. He couldn't help lowering his lips to hers in a soft, welcoming kiss. Her tongue eagerly sought his, releasing his pent-up desire as her hands fisted in his shirt and she rocked her hips against him. He felt his body swell with lust, but it was the slow moan that escaped her lungs and slithered down his throat that did him in.

"Ally." His voice was low, gravelly, and full of lust.

Her eyes blazed, and she deepened the kiss in response. Heath lifted her into his arms and headed for the stairs, ascending them swiftly.

"You're carrying me up the stairs?" she said against his lips with a smile.

"It's quicker." He slowed on the first landing and kissed her again before ascending the remaining stairs to the bedroom, where he set her feet on the floor. Two walls of floor-to-ceiling glass gave way to a glorious view of dark shades of orange, purple, and blue hovering above the city lights and the river below.

"Oh my God. How do you ever sleep? I'd sit here and stare at the view all night long."

The night sky cast a romantic hue into the dark room, silhouetting Ally's curvaceous hips and full breasts. Heath lowered his mouth to the nape of her neck and trailed light kisses to the sensitive spot just below her ear. His hands explored her thighs as he pressed his hard length against her rear.

"You're the only view I want to get lost in, sweetheart."

Her head tipped back with a lusty sigh. She reached behind her and gripped his hips, holding him close as she met his gyrating pelvis with her ass. Heath slowly unzipped her dress and slid it over her shoulders. It fell to the floor in a heap. She was breathing harder, and when Ally pressed her ass against him again, it was all he could do to restrain his carnal desires. He gathered her hair over one shoulder, admiring the graceful lines of her back as he unhooked her bra and gently removed it.

With her back to him, Ally reached behind her, searching for his hips again. He gripped her wrists and held them by her sides as he licked and sucked her neck, then followed the line of her spine with his tongue. He felt her shiver against him as he kissed the dimples at the base of her spine, then laved them with his tongue.

"Heath," she pleaded.

He hooked his fingers in the waistband of her lacy panties and drew them down slowly, then lifted each of her feet to set her free. Bare, save for her black high heels, Ally was a piece of art, shadowed by the light of the moon. Heath knelt behind her, filling his hands with her hips as he licked the curve where her ass met her thighs, loving first one side, then the other, as goose bumps formed on her skin. He ran his hands down one leg, then slowly up, reveling in the feel of her softness, the trust she had in him. His hands traveled north to the juncture of her sex. Heat emanated from between her legs as he swept his thumb over her wet flesh.

She inhaled a sharp breath, spreading her legs to accommodate his large hands, but Heath wasn't in a hurry. He took his time, kissing her perfect, rounded ass and sliding his hands around the front of her hips, holding her in place as he dipped lower and his tongue found the wet, sensitive skin between her legs. Her scent aroused him, and the way her body shivered with every flick of his tongue spurred him on, making his cock throb with need. He felt her fingers move over the swollen, sensitive nub he'd been waiting to taste, and he groaned at the sight of her pleasuring herself. He rose to his full height and stripped bare, pressing his throbbing heat against the seam of her ass as she continued to stroke herself. With one hand clutching her waist, he reached around with the other and buried his fingers deep inside her.

"Heath. Oh God," Ally cried out.

He ground his hips against her ass while furtively seeking the orgasm he knew she needed. He clamped his teeth on the curve of her shoulder, stroking over her most sensitive spot with his fingers. Her thighs tightened against him as the orgasm claimed her. He wrapped one hand around her waist, still teasing with the other, until the last of her climax shuddered through her. Then he reached down and put his hard cock between her legs, rubbing against her swollen sex without penetrating her.

"I have to feel you against me."

He thrust against her ass, her juices coating every inch of his eager cock.

"Oh God, Heath. That feels so good."

She reached between her legs and pressed his shaft against her sex, moaning and driving him out of his fucking mind. He pinched her nipples. *Hard.* And she cried out again, a loud, indiscernible sound that ricocheted off the glass walls and sent a shiver down his spine.

"Too much?" he asked against her cheek.

"More. Harder," she pleaded.

He squeezed harder, and she arched into his hands.

"Fuck, Ally, I need you." He reached for his pants. "Condom."

"No. No condom."

Heath stilled.

"Take me, Heath. I'm on the pill, and you said you've always used protection. So have I."

She moved forward and pressed her hands against the dresser, spreading her legs wide. Heath stroked his cock, and when she looked over her shoulder, her hair sexily covering one eye, her legs spread wide, her ass perched high from her heels, he nearly came.

"I love to see you touch yourself," she said in a heady voice. She reached between her legs again, and that was it.

Heath abandoned all restraint. In one hard thrust he pushed into her. They both moaned with pleasure.

"Ally, you're so wet, so tight. So fucking hot." He thrust in harder, wanting to bury himself as deep as he possibly could, fill every inch of her. Another hard pump brought the sound of flesh slapping against flesh. "Jesus. Tell me if I hurt you."

She spread her hands and legs wider, bending farther over

the dresser as he sank into her, time and time again. He wrapped one arm around her waist, trapping her against him, and groped her breast with the other as her muscles contracted around him.

"Oh…God." Her head fell between her shoulders.

Heath raised her, so her back was pressed to his chest, as her body shook and her hips thrust.

"That's it baby." Every fast pulse brought him closer to his release. She felt amazing as he palmed her breast, while he was buried deep inside her.

As she came down from her orgasm, he lightly kissed her cheek.

"Oh my God. Heath."

She pressed her ass against him again, and he withdrew from inside her and turned her in his arms, taking her in a demanding kiss. She returned his efforts with fervor. They were so in sync sexually that Heath had a hard time thinking straight. He gripped her ass as he ravaged her mouth. She cupped his balls, nearly sending him over the edge, and then she dropped to her knees and took him in her mouth.

"Oh…fuck…." His head tipped back with a growl as his hips plunged forward, thrusting into her mouth over and over again. He felt his release building and wanted—*needed*—to be inside her. He fisted his hands in her hair and moved his hips back.

She gazed up at him, and he lifted her into his arms and lowered her onto his throbbing heat.

"Ah, yes…" she said in a heated breath.

He pulled off her heels and gritted his teeth against the insane pleasure of her legs wrapping tightly around him, her nails digging into his shoulders. He crossed the room and lowered her down to the bed, feeling the heat of their bodies joining again as they hit the mattress. She closed her eyes, and he found her hands and laced their fingers together beside her head.

"Open your eyes, sweetheart."

Her heavy lids lifted, and her lips curved up.

"I adore you," he whispered as his lips found hers again, and he breathed his love into her as their bodies moved in perfect harmony.

Ally awakened every bit of him. His body was on fire, electrified, and as she came apart beneath him and he surrendered to his own powerful release, it was love that filled his veins.

They lay tangled together on their sides in the wake of their lovemaking while their breathing returned to normal.

"Stay with me," he whispered.

She pressed her lips to his, and he pulled her in closer.

"Will you catch me?" she whispered with a sweet smile as she traced his collarbone with her finger.

He furrowed his brow in confusion.

"When I fall for you," she answered. "Will you be there to catch me?"

"For the rest of your life, sweetheart. Day or night." He gathered her in his arms and sealed his vow with a kiss.

Chapter Seventeen

ALLY'S MOTHER USED to tell her that people didn't find love, love found them, and it almost always seemed to do so in the most unusual ways and at the most unlikely times. Her parents had met in high school, and as her mother told the story, she'd hated her father at first sight. He was too full of himself, and he looked at her as if she were *his* when she couldn't imagine ever *wanting* to be his. That was, until he'd found out that she wasn't interested, and he'd spent the next few weeks showing her the person he really was. He'd walked her to every class, even when it meant being late to his own, and every day after school he waited for her in the library, where he knew she went to do her homework. He had inserted himself into her life without an invitation, and despite her mother turning him down for every date for the first month, he was relentless and proved himself as the loving, loyal, smart man Ally knew him to be. And only after he'd stopped being overly cocky and had shown his kind and sensitive self, had she accepted a date—and within a few more weeks, he'd *become* her mother's life. In all the times Ally had heard the story, she'd never put much value in the *I'm not what I seem* scenario, and she'd certainly never linked it to herself in any way. Until now.

As the Saturday-morning sun crept over the horizon and showered her and Heath in a bright new day, she began to see herself differently. When she inched back against him, his chest hair tickled her skin and his hips and thighs cradled her rear, and she realized that the person she'd presented herself as when she'd met Heath wasn't her true self, even though she'd thought it was.

It was who she'd pretended to be—even to herself.

In college Ally had taken the walk of shame once or twice; only she'd never considered it a walk of *shame*. She'd done what *she'd* wanted to do, on *her* terms. After college—and after being cheated on for a second time—she'd stopped wanting anything remotely close to a monogamous relationship. That was when she'd taken control of her personal life. Erecting a wall around herself, sleeping with an occasional man *on her terms*. She realized now that part of her terms meant without any ties to her *true* self. It had been her way of protecting her heart. Heath had somehow touched her in a way that made her want to break through that facade in the same way her father had removed his emotional armor for her mother.

In his sleep, Heath's warm, even breaths whispered across her shoulder. She felt his heart beating against her back, and even in sleep he held her protectively, with one strong arm around her waist. Ally hadn't ever thought of herself as the type of woman who needed protecting, but every ounce of her loved the way Heath had made her *his*. She loved the way he devoured her sexually and the way she caught him stealing glances, as if he might see some hidden piece of her when she wasn't aware that he was looking. Even the way he called her *sweetheart* made her heart squeeze and her belly get warm. As she lay within his embrace, she wondered what she'd been so afraid of. She tried to dissect it, to figure it out as she did the blood work and biopsies she analyzed at work.

Strangely, it wasn't the fear of being cheated on that rushed to the forefront of her mind. That was the one thing she'd always thought she was trying to avoid. But as Heath's arm tightened around her, she knew that wasn't her greatest fear. Her greatest fear was allowing herself to feel the emotions she'd never felt before and the worries that came along with them.

She was falling head over heels in love with Heath. Love, like liquid, had infiltrated her entire being, joining with her blood and settling into her bones, saturating her so completely that she knew she couldn't easily shake it off or pretend it didn't exist. Not that she wanted to do either. But the sense of realness, the sense of complete and utter belonging, was upon her.

If she gave in to these intense emotions and let the last of her resolve go, would Heath *really* always be there to catch her? Or, like wayward cells, would their feelings change into something ugly and unstoppable?

"What're you thinking about?" Heath asked as he rolled Ally onto her back. Sleep hovered in his blue eyes, and a curious smile played across his cheeks.

"Us," she answered honestly.

"Mm. Well, you didn't take off in the middle of the night—that's a good sign."

She smiled. "You held on to me all night like a seat belt."

He pulled her side against his warm skin. "Too confining?"

"Not in the least. I slept great."

"Then why do I sense something serious brewing in your mind?"

This was another part of Heath she was completely drawn to. He paid such careful attention to her that even when she thought there was no way he could notice anything out of the ordinary, he did.

"You know how all it takes is one aberrant cell to destroy a person?"

"Yes." He pushed up on one elbow, and his gaze turned serious.

"All it takes to destroy a relationship is one rogue thought. Or one wrong move. Or…"

"Or someone not really caring enough to protect it?" he asked.

She shifted her eyes away with the truth of his question.

"Isn't that what relationships really come down to?" Heath gently drew her chin toward him, so she had no choice but to look at him. "With illness, control is an illusion. You can eat right and exercise, stay away from cigarettes and alcohol, and still a cancerous cell can turn into many and steal a person's life." He paused, and his eyes softened as he brushed his finger over her cheek.

She loved that he took his time to intimately touch her in the middle of an important thought. He wasn't in a rush to move past her worries or to convince her of his beliefs. It was these little things—the way her thoughts were important to him, the way he cared for her—that were making her *his*.

"The difference is that in relationships, we have full control," he explained. "We make our decisions. Sometimes we make good decisions, sometimes bad decisions, but we're *always* in control of what those decisions are."

She sighed, hating and loving in equal measure the truth of what he'd said.

"Allyson, we've both been on the hurtful side of other people's bad decisions. I can't speak for you, but at thirty-four years old, with a stable and enjoyable career, and a family I love, there's no reason for me to bring someone else into my life unless I *want* that person there and, more importantly, unless I'm willing to do whatever it takes to do the right thing by them."

He gazed into her eyes as she processed what he'd said, and when he spoke again, his tone was even more sincere.

"I want you in my life, Ally, and I don't have a history of making bad decisions. That being said, don't drive yourself crazy picking apart what might happen in our relationship. We're not fortune-tellers, and there are no guarantees, but I can promise you this. The same way I don't give up on helping my patients, I'd never give up on us. If we hit a rough spot that you don't want to ride over, we'll find a way around it. If we hit a snag that seems like it has the power to derail us completely, we'll take a deep breath and think it through. We're both smart, caring people. I'll never take a detour that involves another woman. I've never cheated on a woman in my life."

"I've never cheated on a boyfriend, either."

"Then tell me what really scares you, because falling asleep with you in my arms and waking up with you is something I want to get used to."

"Heath…" She didn't have an answer about what scared her. He'd tamped down her worry with reason and those warm, sensitive eyes of his. "You weren't looking for a relationship, remember?"

"Neither were you," he reminded her. "Do you *not* want this?"

"Oh, no! I want this in the worst way," she assured him. "I just don't want to be taken by surprise by a wayward cell. There are things about me that you don't know. You may not like my bad habits."

"Lay 'em on me, sweetheart. What're your bad habits?" He ran his finger from her ribs to her hip, sending goose bumps over her skin.

"I cry at commercials," she admitted.

"I have tissues." He brought her hand to his mouth and kissed her palm.

"I like to do the Sunday crossword, and sometimes I talk to myself and get angry when I'm doing it."

"I'll get mad with you," he offered with a sweet smile.

"You didn't notice, but I have *three* cat boxes for Fifi, and sometimes I let her sleep on my pillow."

He moved over her and nudged her legs open with his knees. "I'll change the cat boxes for her and buy another pillow so we always have room for her."

She laughed softly. "Sometimes I talk to Amanda on the phone for an hour or more."

He kissed her neck. "Sometimes I spend hours with my brothers." He filled his palms with her breasts and brushed his thumbs over her nipples, making it hard for her to concentrate.

"I eat ice cream from the container."

"I'll fight you for it." He laved his tongue over her nipple, sending ripples of pleasure through her. "Spend the day with me and let me discover everything I don't know about you."

"I have to go home and feed Fifi."

He kissed his way down her belly. "I'll go with you, and we can go out from there." Heath nipped at her inner thighs with his teeth.

She rocked her hips, wanting his mouth on her, wanting him in her.

"I said I'll catch you when you fall." His voice was filled with desire as he splayed his hands over her thighs and used his thumbs to tease her wet, swollen flesh. "All you have to do is let yourself go."

Little did he know she already had one leg over the cliff, and every minute they spent together made her want to propel herself over the edge.

Chapter Eighteen

"I CAN'T BELIEVE I'm here." Ally spun around with her arms wide open, like an enthusiastic little girl.

They'd arrived at Coney Island twenty minutes ago, and Ally had already said the same thing about ten times. Heath would never tire of seeing the spark in her eyes.

"I've lived so close all my life, and never once have I been here." She threw her arms around his neck and kissed him. "Thank you!"

He laughed as he lifted her off her feet and hugged her, and when he set her back down on the ground, she pointed toward the rides. "Let's start there. I've always wanted to go on those swings."

Even though it was early September, the amusement park was crowded and the air was alive with excitement from wide-eyed children and adults holding hands. As they walked around the park, Ally marveled at everything—the rides, the people, the food—and seeing her so happy made Heath want to do more for her. He wanted to take her everywhere and show her the world. He wanted to experience life with her.

"Have you been on that roller coaster?" she asked, pointing to the Cyclone, a roller coaster in the distance.

"Sure, with my brothers." They held hands as they reached the line for the swings.

Ally shaded her eyes from the sun and watched the swings rise toward the sky, then whirl overhead. "That's so much higher and faster than I anticipated."

"Do you want to skip it?" he asked.

"No way." Her smile lit up her beautiful face.

Heath loved the way her eyes took on a challenging gaze. She bent to fix the cuff of her distressed jeans, looking sexier than hell in a pair of cute sandals with a coral-colored, loose-fitting sleeveless top. She turned to look at a laughing child, and her silver earrings sparkled against her dark hair. She tucked her hair behind her ear, and the silver bangles she wore *clinked*, setting her movements to music. Heath would be happy spending the afternoon just watching Ally take in the sights, sounds, and scents of the park.

By the time it was their turn, she was gripping his hand so tightly that he was sure she'd leave fingerprints.

"Are you sure you're okay to do this?" he asked.

She nodded enthusiastically, her eyes wide. "Definitely."

He helped her into her swing and kissed her before claiming the swing beside her.

"I wish we could hold hands while we rode these," she said.

"We'll make up for it later."

As the ride lifted them above the crowd, Ally clung tightly to the red protective sheathing on the metal chains attached to the chair. Heath watched her muscles flex as she tightened her grip, and when the ride picked up speed and her swing arced out and angled slightly sideways, she closed her eyes and tilted her chin up toward the sky. She released the chains and held her arms out to her sides, as if reaching for brass rings, and tipped her head back. Heath couldn't remember ever having witnessed such unencumbered joy. Her hair waved behind her like a thick mane, and when the ride slowed, she looked over at him with rosy cheeks.

When they touched down, she kicked her feet excitedly.

"That was amazing!"

He helped her from her seat, and she jumped into his arms and kissed him as other passengers weaved around them toward the exit. He drank in her exhilaration. He'd forgotten what it felt like to do something like that for the first time, and he realized that what she felt over the ride, he felt being with her.

They laughed and talked as they made their way deeper into the park. Two children scampered by with cotton candy, and Ally's eyes lit up.

"I want that sugary goodness." She pulled Heath toward a cotton candy vendor, and he couldn't help but laugh.

"I haven't had this since I was a kid." Heath ordered a cotton candy and paid while Ally pulled a hunk off.

"Me, either. But I'd eat it for breakfast if I knew how to make it." She put the pink fluff into her mouth and closed her eyes. "Mm. This is better than sex."

"What?" Heath plucked off a hunk and put it in his mouth. "Mm. That's really good, but I'm not sure it's better than sex."

"Oh, come on," Ally teased as she pulled off another hunk and shoved it into his mouth. "Tell me that's not orgasmic."

He tugged her against him and took her in a sloppy, sugary kiss. The cotton candy melted in their mouths, and they both came away laughing.

"Maybe if I were eating it *off of you*…" He arched a brow and licked a sticky speck of pink from the corner of her mouth.

"Dr. Wild, what are you suggesting?" She narrowed her eyes and gave him a limp-wristed wave.

"Exactly what you think I am." He kissed her again and

realized a woman and her young boys were watching them. He draped his arm around Ally, and they walked toward the rides, chuckling and kissing.

The scents of hot dogs and fried foods hung in the air as the afternoon wore on, and the blue sky darkened with the setting sun. They'd ridden the bumper cars, the Ferris wheel, and the roller coaster and had spent hours exploring the park and people watching. They were heading for the beach to stroll along the shore when Heath was drawn in by the lights and sounds of the arcades.

"Don't waste your money," Ally said. "No one ever wins these things."

"Didn't you see all those people carrying stuffed animals? Of course you can win, and I happen to be a master at this stuff. Pick a prize and I'll win it for you." Heath nodded toward the bank of arcades. He'd spent so many hours playing these games with his brothers that he'd learned all the tricks of the trade. Like how he had to toss the basketball high and dead center or it would bounce off the rim, and when playing the squirt gun target game, one movement away from center would cost him the match.

Ally crossed her arms and surveyed the prizes at the water gun shooting game.

"I have a better idea. How about if you win the stuffed cat so Fifi has a friend?" he suggested.

"Me? I can't win anything. You do it. I'll watch."

Heath shook his head. "There's nothing you can't do if you try." He took out his wallet and paid for Ally's turn. "It's easy. All you have to do is aim and shoot. As you hit the target with your stream of water, the monkey climbs the tree. The first one up wins."

Two teenagers were egging each other on beside them as they paid and got ready to play.

Heath moved behind Ally and put the gun in her hand.

"I'm seriously going to suck. You might as well have thrown your money into the ocean." Ally held up the gun and looked nervously at the teens, who had gone silent and serious, standing with their legs shoulder width apart, arms outstretched, reaching forward, and clasping their guns.

Heath pressed his cheek to Ally's from behind. "The key is to find the right spot on the target, then not to move. Don't look at them and don't get distracted by noises. Look, aim, fire."

Ally shrugged. "Okay, but I'm telling you…"

The guy behind the counter sounded a buzzer that counted down 3, 2, 1, then buzzed again.

Ally held down the trigger. Heath held her wobbly arms steady as the hard stream of water pelted the target.

"We're doing it!" she hollered, then looked over at the teens and tilted the gun, missing the target for a split second, which cost them the round. "Aw! Let's do it again. I can do better."

The teenagers hooted and hollered as they chose their prize.

Heath laughed as he paid again, and two more players joined them.

"We've got this." Ally spread her legs wider and held the gun with two hands, her eyes narrowed, focused on the target.

Heath smiled at her concentration. "That's my competitive girl." He stepped back and let her do it on her own.

When the kid beside her won, she whipped her head around to Heath with a challenging look in her eyes. "Again?"

He laughed and paid for another round. "Want me to try?"

"I've got this." She lowered her chin, aimed, and when the

buzzer sounded, she hit the target dead-on, without wobbly arms and without looking away for even a second. Her monkey climbed to the top of the tree and her bell sounded.

"We did it!" Ally jumped up and down and flew into Heath's arms again.

"No, babe. *You* did it."

Ally chose her prize and hugged the stuffed cat to her chest, beaming as they crossed the boardwalk toward the beach. "I've never won anything before, and I wouldn't even have tried if it weren't for you."

"You were a natural."

"A natural, huh? I wonder what I could do with a real gun," she teased.

"I'd much rather see what you can do with cotton candy." He pulled her in close. "I have a feeling that you have the ability to master whatever you put that brilliant mind of yours to. Now, if I could only figure out how to get your sights set on me."

He jumped from the boardwalk down to the beach and reached up to help Ally.

"I've got you in my crosshairs, Dr. Wild," she said as she leaped off the boardwalk and into his arms.

Without missing a step, Heath spun her around and kissed her, knowing he was her easiest target yet.

Chapter Nineteen

THEY WALKED ALONG the shore and had dinner at a café before heading back toward the city. Ally watched the lights move slowly by as they inched along the busy city streets. She couldn't remember the last time she'd had this much fun, and as Heath reached across the console and took her hand in his, she didn't want the night to end.

"It's hard to believe it's only been a few hours since we left your place this morning. I feel like we spent a week at Coney Island." Ally traced a vein in his hand.

"Is that good or bad?"

Ally sighed. "Very good. Do you want to stay at my place tonight?"

Heath smiled, his eyes never leaving the road. "Do you even have to ask?"

She rested her head back and closed her eyes, reveling in the sincerity of his answer and the way it made her pulse quicken. She listened to his breathing hitch, as if he swallowed a laugh, and when she opened her eyes, he was grinning ear to ear.

"Why do you look so happy?"

"Because you're letting me in." He brought her hand to his mouth and pressed a kiss to it.

"I think I let you in the first night I met you," she reminded him with a playful smirk.

"Yes, but now you're letting me into Ally's private oasis. There's a world of difference."

They stopped at his place so Heath could pick up a change of clothes and drop off his car. Ally was pleased that this time he didn't mind showing her how he really lived. She'd heard about the fancy garage units. Probably everyone in the city had, it was so elaborate, but Heath acted as though it was just like any old garage, and she appreciated that. During the cab ride over to her apartment, Ally wondered if her apartment would feel confining after sleeping at Heath's, and was pleasantly surprised that it didn't feel any less beautiful than it ever had. Heath moved through her place with comfort, toeing off his shoes by the front door and setting his wallet and keys by the bed. He picked up Fifi and snuggled her for a few minutes while Ally took off her sandals and gave Fifi fresh food and water.

A few minutes later the activity of the day caught up with them, and they both collapsed onto the couch. Heath stretched out with Ally beside him, and when Fifi sniffed around his feet, he lifted her onto his chest, where she promptly curled up and fell asleep.

Several hours later Ally awoke in her bed with a soft blanket draped over her. The apartment was pitch-dark, and the clock on the bedside table read 3:00 a.m. She drank in Heath looking deliciously handsome, sprawled across her bed with only a sheet strewn across his hips and Fifi curled up against his chest. Ally's hand covered her heart. She felt her life falling into place. Sometime between Saturday morning and this moment, she'd become wholly *Heath's*. She was completely in love with him. She sat there for a few minutes, savoring the sight of his big, strong body snuggling her kitty, and when her body finally remembered how to move, she rose to her feet feeling like she was walking on a cloud.

Changing into a negligee, she wondered how things could move so quickly—from the way she breathed to the weight of the air in the apartment. She went into the bathroom to brush her teeth and saw Heath's toothbrush hanging in the ceramic holder beside hers. A damp towel hung over the towel rack. She touched it and felt her heart squeeze. She was bummed to have missed the opportunity to shower with Heath and delighted at the thought of him making himself at home in her apartment. She peeked behind the shower curtain, imagining him going quietly through the motions of his nighttime routine while trying not to wake her. She wondered if he'd talked to Fifi, the way she did as she got ready for bed each night. She saw his shampoo, body wash, and shaving cream in a toiletry bag on her sink. His razor was sticking out of the top. Seeing all those things sent a tingle through her limbs that spread like wildfire around her heart.

She loved seeing Heath's things mingling with hers, and when she walked back into the bedroom, her heart nearly stopped at the sight of him. His eyes were partway open. He held a finger up to his lips to shush her and pointed to Fifi sleeping soundly against him; then he opened his hand for her to take. She slid into the bed carefully, and he blew her a silent kiss.

"Sorry I fell asleep," she whispered.

"You were adorable, and I had good company." He beckoned her closer.

Ally inched closer, until Fifi was nestled safely between them, and for the first time in her life, she wondered what it might be like to have a child. Amanda was the dreamer in the family. Ally had never given much thought to marriage or babies, but now, as sleep made her eyelids heavy, her mind drifted to what it might be like to be married to Heath. To have a family of their own. Heath smiled as he curled one hand around her and laid the other protectively over Fifi. He had such a big heart, and as her eyes rolled over his contented expression and he gathered them both in close, she imagined he'd make a loving and protective father.

"Good night, sweetheart," he whispered.

A minute later his chest rose and fell in the even pattern of sleep, and Ally's heart beat a little harder.

Chapter Twenty

ALLY AWOKE TO the sound of Fifi purring. She felt the weight of Heath lying a few inches away on the mattress, and when she opened her eyes, she found him petting Fifi.

"Hi, sleepyhead." He leaned over Fifi and kissed her.

"You didn't mind that she slept here?"

He lifted Fifi onto his bare chest, and the kitty licked his chin. "This little muffin? Not at all." He reached one arm out and pulled Ally closer. "I have my two favorite girls in bed with me."

She smiled and petted Fifi. "She's very spoiled."

"She's very loved. There's a difference." He kissed Ally's forehead, laid his head back on the pillow, and closed his eyes. "What do you usually do Sunday mornings?"

"Depends. Sometimes I lie around and read all morning."

"That sounds luxurious." He smiled and opened his eyes.

"You mean *lazy*."

He laughed.

"I'm not always lazy. Sometimes I go for a run. Gosh, I haven't been since I got back from Vermont. I should really get out of bed and go running."

"You're a runner?" Heath pushed up on one elbow, sliding Fifi back onto the mattress. The kitty yawned and stretched her front paws out, pressing her butt up in the air. Then she leaped from the mattress to the floor.

"A *jogger*. I'm not very fast."

"Let's go for a run together," he suggested. "I run a few times each week. We have more in common than we even imagined."

"You'll blow me away. Your legs are much longer than mine, and I'm sure you're much faster."

"Come on. I'll go slow."

Before she could answer, his cell phone rang.

"That's the answering service ring tone." He sat up to answer the call. "Yes." He paused, and while he listened, he rose to his feet and reached for his bag of clothes. "I'll be right there." He ended the call and pulled on his briefs.

"One of my patients has been in an accident." He pulled on his shirt and spoke fast. "I have to go to the hospital."

As he pulled on his socks, Ally grabbed his shoes from the living room and brought them to him. "I hope your patient's okay."

He shoved his feet into his shoes, and Ally handed him his wallet and keys as he headed for the door. "I'm sorry, sweetheart. Go for your run. Do something fun today. I'm not sure how long I'll be, but I'll call you later, when I have a handle on things."

She unlocked the door, and he pulled her into his arms.

"Are we still on for dinner with my family?" He smiled. "Even though that makes me sound like a mama's boy?"

"I *love* the mama's boy in you."

Heath's piercing blue eyes narrowed, and a smile spread across his lips.

"I mean...I *like*...I mean..." *Love. I mean I love everything about you.*

"You mean?"

"I…"

He sealed his lips over hers and took her in a knee-weakening kiss, and when their lips parted, he searched her eyes with a glint of hope in his.

"You have to go." *Before I say* I love you. She took a step back, afraid she'd melt against him and her feelings would flow like a river from her lips.

"Yes, I do. And when I see you later, you can tell me *exactly* what you mean." He pressed two fast kisses to her lips, then went out the door and called over his shoulder, "Love you, sweethe—"

Ally sucked in a breath.

Heath stopped, as if the words had rolled off his tongue without thought and shocked him, too. He turned, and the confused look on his face quickly morphed into a wide smile. He pulled her in close again, breathing hard.

"I have to leave, but I do love you, Ally. And I mean *exactly* that." With another quick kiss, he hurried down the hall to the elevator, turning to look at her as the doors slid open.

"Pick your jaw up off the floor." He blew her a kiss and disappeared into the elevator.

Ally stood stock-still for a few seconds, her mind a frantic tangle of thoughts all circling one big truth: *I love you, too, Heath.*

She ran inside and tugged on a pair of sweats, shoved her feet into her sneakers, snagged her keys, and ran into the hall. She pushed through the stairwell doors and flew down to the lobby, bursting through the entrance to her building in time to see Heath climbing into a cab.

"Heath!" She ran into the street, dressed in her negligee and sweatpants, with a major case of bed head, and leaped into his arms. "You caught me, just like you said you would."

"I always will," he said with a wide smile.

"I love you, too, Heath. And I mean *exactly* that." She kissed him quickly and wiggled out of his strong arms, then gave him a playful shove toward the cab. "Pick your jaw up off the ground and go. Your patient needs you."

"God, I love you," he said as he climbed into the cab.

She watched his cab disappear into the mass of cars moving down the busy street, and when she turned back toward her apartment building, a small crowd had gathered. They whistled and clapped, and rather than shrink back in embarrassment, Ally took a bow before heading into her building.

Her heart raced as she walked into her apartment and scooped Fifi into her arms.

"I love him, Fifi. I do. I love him."

Fifi meowed.

"I know. You do, too. I could tell."

She was headed for the bathroom with an unstoppable grin on her face and her heart dancing in her chest, when her cell phone rang. She saw Heath's name on the screen, and before she could say hello, he said, "Tell me again."

"Go. Your patient needs you," she teased.

He laughed. "Tell me, Ally."

"I love your smile, and your voice, and the way you look at me like I'm the only person you see. I love the way you hold me and the way you touch me. I love how you love your family, and I love how you treat Fifi. I love all of you, Heath. The good, the bad, and the naughty. Maybe especially the naughty."

"Ally?"

Her belly fluttered at his seductive tone. "Yes?"

"I've waited my whole life for you. Loving me will be the best decision you've ever made, sweetheart. I'll never let you down."

She sank down to her bed thinking of the night they'd met, the way he'd stroked her hand instead of her thigh when they were in the bar. How, as they'd gotten closer, he'd told her how important his family was to him. Seeing him with his family had confirmed what she'd known from the start—Heath was a man who knew how to respect a woman—and what she'd known from the moment their lips had touched and from the way he'd treated her every minute since—Heath knew how to *love* a woman.

"The second best decision of my life," she said. "The first was accepting your invitation the night we met."

Epilogue

ALLY TIDIED UP the bed and stretched, reveling in the glow of the moon streaking in through the bedroom windows. She heard Heath downstairs moving about, and Fifi was asleep on *her* pillow. Ally and Heath had been living together for five weeks, and true to his word, Heath had changed Fifi's cat boxes, of which she now had seven to accommodate her needs on each floor and in each of the spacious rooms. It was a Sunday evening, and she and Heath were going to watch his brothers Jackson and Cooper hold a photo shoot in Washington Square Park. Ally slipped on her boots and grabbed a sweater. Fall, her favorite season, had officially arrived.

She gave Fifi a light pet, then headed downstairs, where she found Heath in the kitchen, looking incredibly sexy in a pair of dark jeans and a black cashmere sweater. He opened his arms, and she snuggled in, still feeling like she was living in a dream.

"Good evening, beautiful." He kissed her softly, and she went up on her toes for another. "Are you almost ready to go?"

"I'm ready. I want to call Amanda. She hasn't returned my calls all day."

"Can you call her on the way?" Heath asked as they headed for the door.

"Sure."

Heath opened the foyer closet and pulled out one of Ally's

colorful scarves.

"It's chilly tonight." He wrapped it gently around her neck, then kissed her forehead.

He'd become even more thoughtful and caring since they'd vowed their love for each other. Ally had never felt so cherished in all her life. Heath had remained just as communicative as he'd always been, calling if he was running late and offering to stop on his way home to pick up groceries or cat food. Every Sunday they had dinner with his family, and Heath's mom and Ally's parents had hit it off when her parents had gone to Mary Lou's for dinner last weekend.

Outside, the air was brisk, and the sounds of leaves whisking in the wind was musical as they entered the park. A breeze swept along the ground, sending leaves into a flurry along their path. Heath pulled Ally against him to shield her from the cold. Ally tried to reach Amanda and had to leave a message.

"No luck, huh?"

"No. I'm getting worried. She always at least texts me back."

"What are you worried about? She's a big girl." Heath tightened his grip as a group of teenagers walked by.

"I don't know. She had that date last night, and she said the guy was a jerk. I'm sure I'm overthinking."

She shoved her phone in her pocket. "Can we stop by her place after the shoot? Just to check on her?"

Heath kissed her forehead as they neared the fountain. "Of course, sweetheart. Whatever you want."

Several people were taking pictures around the fountain; others were marveling at the colorful lights or cuddling on the concrete steps by the water. In the center of the wide round fountain, water spouted straight up in the air, illuminated from below by colorful lights, which gave the fountain—and the night—a celebratory feel. Water arced high in the air around the circumference of the fountain and fell in beautiful sprays into the stepped pool of the fountain below.

"Heath, look how beautiful it is tonight. I don't know if I've ever seen colored lights on the fountain. I guess Jackson and Cooper had that done for the photo shoot?" She looked around.

"They must have."

A breeze swept droplets of water across their cheeks. Ally pressed her face to Heath's chest and laughed. His strong arms circled her and held her close.

A tall, dark-haired man carrying two bouquets of roses and a bunch of balloons walked up behind Heath, then stopped beside him.

"Hi," Heath said.

Ally had learned a lot about Heath over the past few weeks, and one of the things she admired was his friendliness toward strangers.

"Hi. I'm supposed to meet my girlfriend here, and I need to grab something from over there." He pointed to where a group of people were standing a few feet away. He was nicely dressed, in a pair of slacks and a sweater covered by a light jacket. "Would you mind holding these for a moment?"

"Sure." Heath took the flowers and the man handed Ally the balloons.

"Thank you. I'll be right back." The man went back the way he'd come.

"That was weird." Ally peered around Heath at the man, now talking with a group of friends a few feet away.

The man didn't appear to be coming back, or at least he was taking his dear old time, laughing and talking while Ally and Heath held his goodies.

"Oh my God, Heath. What is he doing? I feel like I'm on *Candid Camera*."

Heath handed her the flowers. "Can you hold these for one sec? I want to call Cooper and see where they are." He put the bouquets in Ally's hands, then put his hand in his coat pocket as she tried to juggle the balloons and flowers.

"Hurry. I'm afraid I'll drop them."

Heath dropped to one knee and looked up at her.

She rolled her eyes. "What are you doing?"

Heath withdrew his hand from his pocket and smiled up at Ally. "Allyson Jenner, you have turned my world upside down. You've filled my heart and my home with love—"

"Oh my God. Heath. Oh my God. Are you…?" Her eyes welled with tears as her mother, father, and sister came out of the shadows behind Heath, setting those tears free. She tried to cover her gaping jaw and managed to smack herself in the face with the roses. "Ohmygodohmygod."

Tears streamed down her face as Heath's brothers and mother came into view over his other shoulder.

"Heath," she whispered.

"Ally, I love you, and I want to spend the rest of my life with you and Fifi and as many babies as you want to have." He took her hand in his, and her legs turned to wet noodles, dropping her to her knees.

She heard Amanda and her mother say her name, and a collective gasp sounded behind Heath, but it was all muffled as Heath caught her and helped her find stability. There they crouched, Ally holding a fistful of balloons and armfuls of roses and Heath gazing into her eyes like she was his whole world— just as he was hers. A lump formed in Ally's throat, stealing her ability to speak. In her peripheral vision she saw flashes of light from Cooper's and Jackson's cameras.

As tears slid down her cheeks, she found Heath's loving gaze.

"You caught me," she said just above a whisper, tasting the salty tears as they slipped over her lips.

"I promised I would for the rest of your life, sweetheart, day or night. I never lie." He held a ring between his finger and thumb. Diamonds glistened in the moonlight as he picked up her left hand and helped her reposition the flowers in her arms.

"Ally?"

"Mm-hm?" *Ohgodohgodohgod.*

"Ally, will you marry me?"

Yes! Yes! She opened her mouth to say yes, but no words came.

She cleared her throat, feeling their family members step in closer. Into their bubble of love. Into the rest of her life.

Into the rest of our life.

"Yes. Yes, Heath, I'll marry you." She flung herself into his arms, crushing the flowers between them as the balloons floated up into the night sky.

He sealed his lips over hers as cheers and congratulations sounded around them.

"Marrying me will be the second best decision you've ever made, sweetheart," Heath said against her lips.

"Third," she reminded him. "But who's counting?"

Heath hugged her, and over Heath's shoulder Ally eyed Amanda, who was also in tears, hugging their mother.

"I couldn't answer your calls," Mandy called to her. "This was too big. I would have told you!"

Ally laughed as her vision blurred from her tears. With shaky hands she held on to Heath and looked into the piercing blue eyes that'd had her from the moment she'd first seen him walk into the resort in Vermont.

"Come with me." Ally held Heath's hand and walked over to Mary Lou. She took her soon-to-be mother-in-law's hands and pressed them to her cheeks. "Can you feel it?"

"Honey," she answered with damp eyes. "Your love is so big I can see it."

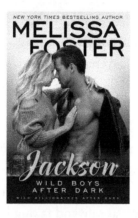

Chapter One

JACKSON WILD PUT his cell phone on speaker mode, set it on the coffee table, and shoved a few extra protein bars into his backpack as he listened to his younger brother and business partner rattle off their schedule for next weekend's photo shoot. They owned one of the most prestigious photography studios in New York City, and both of them enjoyed the perks of the business—leggy models and actresses who loved to party. Jackson had never missed an event, but that didn't stop his overly organized brother, Cooper, from confirming for a second time.

"Sage Remington's gallery opening is Friday night. Are you sure you and Erica will be back by then?"

Jackson flopped onto his leather couch and kicked his bare feet up on the table beside the phone.

"Yeah. We're coming back Thursday night." Gazing out at

the city lights, he thought about Erica Lane, who had been his best friend—*with benefits*—since high school. Everyone except Jackson called her Erica. He'd given her the nickname Laney the very first time they'd met, when she'd been a tough, mouthy, and beautiful teenager.

"You've got Mom covered while I'm away?" Jackson asked. Their father had been killed while trying to ward off an attack on their mother in the middle of the night, right in their bedroom. He'd rushed the attacker, but he was no match for the two bullets that tore through his chest and stole his life as his wife suffered a savage beating that left her blind. Now Jackson and his three brothers took turns visiting their mother on a daily basis, making sure she was safe and taking her on outings and to run errands, and in general, ensuring she continued to have a full life after losing their father and her eyesight.

"Yeah. No problem," Cooper assured him. "How'd things go with those two girls from the bar you took home Wednesday night? They were smokin' hot."

"Let's just say—" Jackson turned at the sound of his front door flying open and slamming against the doorstop.

"Get your clothes off," Laney hollered as she burst through the door carrying an armful of red roses and the biggest box of chocolates Jackson had ever seen. She slammed the chocolates and roses on the counter. Several roses tumbled to the floor, leaving a trail of petals as Laney glared over her shoulder at him.

"Come on. *Strip*," she demanded. Her blond hair was wild, as if she'd run from wherever she'd come from, and her cheeks were red with anger, but it was the look in her eyes that had Jackson's blood boiling. They were damp, as if she'd been crying.

He strode across the room, forgetting about Cooper, and

grabbed her by the shoulders. She glared up at him with her jaw tight, her eyes shooting daggers as she tore at the buttons on his shirt.

"Get this off. I need to get laid." She was five foot four to his six three, with full, pouty lips, an angular, tipped-up nose, and big hazel eyes, which could look innocent or wicked, depending on her mood. Currently they were watery and angry, which had his gut fisting into a knot. She shifted away from his gaze as she fumbled with his buttons and said, "Fuck. I can't—"

Jackson pressed his hand to hers on his chest and felt her trembling.

"Talk to me, Laney. Why were you crying? What happened?"

"Nothing. I wasn't cryi—" She pulled her top off and wiggled out of her miniskirt, which left her in a pair of black heels, a sexy black lace bra, and matching panties. Jackson had seen her naked and in just about every stage of undress one could imagine hundreds of times, and still, he was rock hard in seconds. She had no idea how hot she was, with full breasts straining against her bra, her taut stomach begging to be licked, and hips made for holding on to while she rode him hard. But Jackson knew just how hot she was. Damn did he know.

She pulled her hand out from beneath his. "Stop gawking and take your clothes off." She ripped open the button on his jeans and fought with the zipper.

He stripped to his skivvies as he said, "Fine, but just tell me if I have to go kick some Ricker ass." Laney had been dating Bryce Ricker for about nine months, and as far as Jackson knew, things were going well—even if she refused to commit to a monogamous relationship with the guy. Her parents had divorced when she was in high school, and ever since, she'd said she'd commit to a man *when hell froze over*, which suited him just fine.

"*No*, you don't have to kick his ass; you just have to fuck tonight out of me." She grabbed his hand and dragged him through the living room toward his bedroom. Her heels tapped out an angry tune against the hardwood floor.

"Laney—"

"Jesus, Jackson. Since when do you talk so much? I'm fine, okay? *Fine*." The harsh clench of her jaw told him she was very far from fine, but he knew that once their bodies came together, she'd be fine in no time, and then she'd spill her guts. And he'd decide for himself if he was kicking Ricker's ass or not.

"Hi, Erica." Cooper's voice sailed up from the cell phone on the coffee table as they passed.

"Cooper?" She stopped cold, and Jackson ran right into her luscious curves. Her eyes shot up to Jackson, then darted around the room.

"Cell phone," Jackson said.

"Damn it, Jackson, you could have told me." Laney's eyes darted back to the phone. "Hi, Coop. Jackson has to go now."

Jackson smirked. His family had known about him and Laney sleeping together since his mother caught them in bed together their senior year in high school. *That was a fun afternoon*, he thought sarcastically, remembering his mother's surprise and the lecture he'd gotten afterward.

Jackson picked up the phone, took it off speaker mode, and pressed it to his ear. "I'll catch ya later, Coop."

"You lucky bastard. Breakup sex?"

He eyed his best friend, whose arms were crossed as she tapped her toes impatiently. "Dunno."

"No, it's not breakup sex!" Laney took the phone from

Jackson, whispering, "You need to lower the volume on your stupid phone." She turned her attention to Cooper. "It's I-can't-think-straight sex. Are you guys cool? Can we hang up now?"

She ended the call and pulled Jackson into the bedroom. The room was dark, save for the lights of the city ten stories below. He gripped Laney's arms and spun her against him, searching her eyes for the truth. Bryce Ricker was a nice guy, a stable stockbroker who treated Laney well. But there was something about the guy that rubbed Jackson the wrong way—he was *too* good. He was *too* nice, and if he did a damn thing to Laney, he'd be *too* dead.

"Tell me he didn't do anything bad, or we're not doing this."

She placed her hands on his hips and stepped in closer, bringing her belly against his throbbing erection, and slid her hands up his rib cage and over his pecs, which were strung tight.

"He didn't do anything bad," she said just above a whisper. "I would never lie to you. I just need..." Her hands traveled down to his ass, and she pulled their bodies flush against each other. "This."

He cupped her beautiful face in his hands and brushed his lips over hers, feeling her anticipation in the arch of her back. He ran his tongue over the sweet bow of her lower lip, then pressed soft kisses to her lips as her hands slipped beneath his briefs and cupped his bare ass.

"Off," she whispered.

He pressed his cheek to hers, knowing exactly how to calm her racing thoughts, and whispered, "In due time."

"Jackson," she said in one long breath.

He lowered his mouth to her neck and sucked in her supple skin, earning a throaty moan.

"Please," she said. "I need you *now*."

"You don't *know* need yet." He pulled her tight against him, grazing his teeth over the ridge of her shoulder. He loved her taste, her softness, and the way her entire body reached for him, from her pert nipples to her rocking hips. Even after more than ten years of having sex whenever the urge struck, every time felt like the first—only better, hotter, because they both knew exactly how to get the other one off.

To continue reading, buy
WILD BOYS AFTER DARK: JACKSON

Now Available
SEIZED BY LOVE (The Ryders)

Chapter One

THERE WERE SOME nights when Lizzie Barber simply didn't feel like donning an apron, black-framed glasses, and high heels, covering her shiny brunette locks with a blond wig, and prancing around nearly naked. Tonight was one of those nights. Gazing at her reflection in the mirror of her basement bathroom, Lizzie tucked the last few strands of her hair beneath the wig and forced her very best smile. Thank God her elfin lips naturally curled up at the edges—even when she wasn't smiling, she looked like she was. And tonight she definitely wasn't in the mood to smile. Her oven had been acting up for the last few nights, and she prayed to the gods of all things sugary and sweet that it would behave tonight.

Tightening the apron tie around her neck and the one around her waist, to avoid wardrobe malfunctions, and tugging on the hem of the apron to ensure her skin-colored thong and all her naughty bits were covered, she went into the studio—aka the miniscule kitchen located in the basement of her cute Cape Cod cottage—and surveyed her baking accoutrements one last time before queuing the intro music for her webcast and pasting that perfectly perky smile back in place.

"Welcome back, my hot and hunky bakers," she purred into the camera. "Today we're going to bake delicious angel food cupcakes with fluffy frosting that will make your mouth water." She leaned forward, flashing the camera an eyeful of cleavage and her most seductive smile as she crooked her finger in a come-hither fashion. "And because we all know it's what's *beneath* all that delicious frosting that counts, we're going to sprinkle a few surprises inside the thick, creamy centers."

Lizzie had mastered making baking sound naughty while in college, when her father had taken ill and her parents had closed their inn for six months to focus on his medical care, leaving Lizzie without college tuition. Her part-time job at a florist shop hadn't done a darn thing for her mounting school loans, and when a friend suggested she try making videos and monetizing them to earn fast cash, she drew upon her passion for baking and secretly put on a webcast called *Cooking with Coeds*. It turned out that scantily clad baking was a real money earner. She'd paid for her books and meal plan that way, and eventually earned enough to pay for most of her college tuition. Lizzie had two passions in life—baking and flowers—and she'd hoped to open her own floral shop after college. After graduation, *Cooking with Coeds* became the *Naked Baker* webcast, and she'd made enough money to finish paying off her school loans and open a flower shop in Provincetown, Massachusetts, just like she'd always dreamed of. She hadn't intended to continue the Naked Baker after opening P-town Petals, but when her parents fell upon hard times again and her younger sister Maddy's educational fund disappeared, the Naked Baker webcast became Lizzie's contribution to Maddy's education. Their very conservative parents would have a conniption if they knew what their proper little girl was doing behind closed doors, but what other choice did she have? Her parents ran a small bed-and-breakfast in Brewster, Massachusetts, and with her father's health ping-ponging, they barely earned enough money to make ends meet—and affording college for a child who had come as a surprise to them seven years after Lizzie was born had proven difficult.

Lizzie narrowed her eyes seductively as she gazed into the camera and stirred the batter. She dipped her finger into the rich, creamy goodness and put that finger into her mouth, making a sensual show of sucking it off. "Mm-mm. Nothing better than *thick, creamy batter*." Her tongue swept over her lower lip as she ran through the motions of creating what she'd come to think of as *baking porn*.

During the filming of each show, she reminded herself often of why she was still doing something that she felt ashamed of and kept secret. There was no way she was going to let her sweet nineteen-year-old sister fend for herself and end up doing God knew what to earn money like she did instead of focusing on her studies. Or worse, drop out of school. Madison was about as innocent as they came, and while Lizzie might once have been that innocent, her determination to succeed, and life circum-stances, had beaten it out of her. Creating the webcast was the best decision she'd ever made—even if it meant putting her nonexistent social life on hold and living a secret life after dark. The blond wig and thick-framed spectacles helped to hide her online persona, or at least they seemed to. No one had ever accused her of being the Naked Baker. Then again, her assumption was that the freaky people who got off watching her prance around in an apron and heels probably rarely left their own basements.

She was proud of helping Maddy. She felt like she was taking one for the team. Going where no girl should ever have to go. Braving the wild naked baking arena for the betterment of the sister she cherished.

A while later, as Lizzie checked the cupcakes and realized that while the oven was still warm, it had turned *off*—her stomach sank. Hiding her worries behind another forced smile and a wink, she stuck her ass out and bent over to quickly remove the tray of cupcakes from the oven, knowing the angle of the camera would give only a side view and none of her bare ass would actually be visible. Thankfully, the oven must have just died, because it was still warm and the cupcakes were firm enough to frost.

Emergency reshoot avoided!

Smile genuine!

A few minutes later she sprinkled the last of the coconut on the cupcakes, narrating as she went.

"Everyone wants a little something extra on top, and I'm going to give it to you *good*." Giving one last wink to the camera, she said, "Until next week, this is your Naked Baker signing off for a sweet, seductive night of tantalizing tasting."

She clicked the remote and turned off the camera. Eyeing the fresh daisies she'd brought home from her flower shop, she leaned her forearms on the counter, and with a heavy sigh, she let her head fall forward. It was after midnight, and she had to be up bright and early to open the shop. Tomorrow night she'd edit the webcast so it would be ready in time to air the following night—*and* she needed to get her oven fixed.

Damn thing.

Kicking off her heels, Lizzie went upstairs, stripped out of the apron, and wrapped a thick towel around herself. A warm shower was just what she needed to wash away the film of shame left on her skin after taping the webcast. Thinking of the broken oven, she texted her friend Blue Ryder to see if he could fix it. Blue was a highly sought after craftsman who worked for the Kennedys and other prominent families around the Cape. When Lizzie's pipe had burst under the sink in the bathroom above the first-floor kitchen while she was away at a floral convention for the weekend, Blue was only too happy to put aside time to handle the renovations. He was like that. Always making time to help others. He was still splitting his time between working on her kitchen renovations and working on the cottage he'd just purchased. He was working at his cottage tomorrow, but she hoped he could fit her in at some point.

Can you fix my oven tomorrow?

Blue texted back a few seconds later. He was as reliable as he was hot, a dangerous combination. She read his text—*Is that code for something sexy?*—and shook her head with a laugh.

Smirking, she replied, *Only if you're into oven grease.*

Blue had asked her out many times since they'd met last year, when she'd handled the flowers for his friends' quadruple beach wedding. Turning down his invitations wasn't easy and had led to more sexy fantasies than she cared to admit. Her double life was crazy enough without adding a sexy, rugged man who was built like Magic Mike and had eyes that could hypnotize a blind woman, but her reasons went far deeper than that. Blue was more than eye candy. He was also a genuine friend, and he always put family and friends first, which, when added to his panty-dropping good looks and gentlemanly demeanor, was enough to stop Lizzie's brain from functioning. It would be too easy to fall hard for a caring, loyal man like Blue Ryder. And *that*, she couldn't afford. Maddy was counting on her.

She read his text—*Glad you finally came to your senses. When are you free?*—and wondered if he thought *she* was being flirtatious.

Time to nip this in the bud, she thought. Her finger hovered over the screen while her mind toyed with images of Blue, six foot three, all hot, hard muscles and steel-blue eyes.

It had been way too long since she'd been with a man, and every time Blue asked her out, she was tempted, but she liked him so much as a friend, and she knew that tipping over from friendship to lovers would only draw her further in to him, making it harder to lead her double life.

That was precisely why she hightailed it out of her house on the mornings before he showed up to work on her kitchen. Leaving before he arrived was the only way she was able to keep her distance. He was *that* good-looking. *That* kind. And *that* enjoyable to be around. Not only didn't she have time for a relationship, but she was pretty sure that no guy would approve of his girlfriend doing the *Naked Baker* show. Of course, the mornings after taping her shows, she left him a sweet treat on the counter with a note thanking him for working on her kitchen.

Even though Blue couldn't see her as she drew back her shoulders and put on her most solemn face, she did it anyway to strengthen her resolve as she typed a text that she hoped would very gently set him straight. *After work, but this is REALLY to fix my oven. The one I cook with! Thank you! See you around seven?*

She set the phone down and stepped into the shower, determined not to think about his blue eyes or the way his biceps flexed every time he moved his arms. Her mind drifted to when she'd arrived home from work yesterday and found Blue bending over his toolbox, his jeans stretched tight across his hamstrings and formed to his perfect ass. Her nipples hardened with the thought. He'd been the man she'd conjured up in her late-night fantasies since last summer. What did it hurt? He'd never know. She closed her eyes and ran her hand over her breasts, down her taut stomach, and between her legs. She may not have time to date, but a little midnight fantasy could go a long way...

To continue reading, buy
SEIZED BY LOVE (The Ryders)

More Books By Melissa

Dreaming of Love
Crashing into Love

THE BRADENS at Peaceful Harbor

Healed by Love
Surrender My Love
River of Love
Crushing on Love
Whisper of Love
Thrill of Love

THE BRADEN NOVELLAS

Promise My Love
Our New Love
Daring Her Love
Story of Love

THE REMINGTONS

Game of Love
Stroke of Love
Flames of Love
Slope of Love
Read, Write, Love
Touched by Love

SEASIDE SUMMERS

Seaside Dreams
Seaside Hearts
Seaside Sunsets
Seaside Secrets
Seaside Nights
Seaside Embrace
Seaside Lovers
Seaside Whispers

BAYSIDE SUMMERS
Bayside Desires

The RYDERS
Seized by Love
Claimed by Love
Chased by Love
Rescued by Love
Thrill of Love

SEXY STANDALONE ROMANCE
Tru Blue
Wild Whiskey Nights

HARBORSIDE NIGHTS SERIES
Includes characters from the Love in Bloom series
Catching Cassidy
Discovering Delilah
Tempting Tristan
Chasing Charley
Breaking Brandon
Embracing Evan
Reaching Rusty
Loving Livi

More Books by Melissa
Chasing Amanda (mystery/suspense)
Come Back to Me (mystery/suspense)
Have No Shame (historical fiction/romance)
Love, Lies & Mystery (3-book bundle)
Megan's Way (literary fiction)
Traces of Kara (psychological thriller)
Where Petals Fall (suspense)

Acknowledgments

If you haven't read the Love in Bloom series yet, then dive in and read about the hot, sexy, and wickedly naughty characters in the Snow Sisters, The Bradens, The Remingtons, Seaside Summers, and The Ryders. You can also look forward to Harborside Nights, The Steeles, and The Stones.

Many thanks to my fans for your constant encouragement and inspiration. I love chatting with you on social media and receiving your emails. To keep up with my writing and chat about our lovable heroes and sassy heroines, follow me on Facebook:

facebook.com/MelissaFosterAuthor

Remember to sign up for my newsletter to keep up-to-date with new releases and special promotions and events:

www.MelissaFoster.com/Newsletter

I am indebted to my amazing team of editors and proofreaders, whose meticulous efforts help bring you the cleanest books possible. Thank you: Kristen Weber, Penina Lopez, Jenna Bagnini, Juliette Hill, Marlene Engel, and Lynn Mullan. Thank you, Elizabeth Mackey, for the gorgeous cover.

Loads of gratitude to my research partner and very best friend, Les.

Melissa Foster is a *New York Times* and *USA Today* bestselling and award-winning author. Her books have been recommended by *USA Today's* book blog, *Hagerstown* magazine, *The Patriot*, and several other print venues. She is the founder of the World Literary Café, and when she's not writing, Melissa helps authors navigate the publishing industry through her author training programs on Fostering Success. Melissa has painted and donated several murals to the Hospital for Sick Children in Washington, DC.

Visit Melissa on her website or chat with her on social media. Melissa enjoys discussing her books with book clubs and reader groups and welcomes an invitation to your event.

Melissa's books are available through most online retailers in paperback and digital formats.

www.MelissaFoster.com